The Legend of Miner's Creek

Bess's eyes widened as Nancy carefully removed the wooden plug. The handle of the pickax was hollow. Nancy reached in and pulled out a brittle, yellowed paper. She gently flattened it out, holding the corners with her fingers. It was a map of Prospector's Canyon!

The girls bent over the map. Nancy held it carefully as Rachel traced the line labeled Miner's Creek. Then Rachel helped pick out landmarks that George and Nancy recognized from their ride to the cliffs that morning. A crevice was shown in the rocks that looked like a shallow cave. A small *X* was drawn in the center of the opening.

"Can we know for sure that this *X* means a gold mine?" Bess asked.

"We can't," Nancy said. "Not without going back to Prospector's Canyon and doing some digging of our own. In the meantime, maybe we can use this map to catch a crook."

Nancy Drew
Mystery Stories

Available from MINSTREL Books

NANCY DREW MYSTERY STORIES®

107

NANCY DREW®

THE LEGEND OF MINER'S CREEK

CAROLYN KEENE

A MINSTREL® BOOK

PUBLISHED BY POCKET BOOKS

New York   London   Toronto   Sydney   Tokyo   Singapore

A MINSTREL PAPERBACK *ORIGINAL*

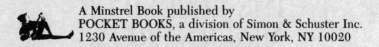

A Minstrel Book published by
POCKET BOOKS, a division of Simon & Schuster Inc.
1230 Avenue of the Americas, New York, NY 10020

Copyright © 1992 by Simon & Schuster Inc.
Front cover illustration by Aleta Jenks
Produced by Mega-Books of New York, Inc.

ISBN: 0-671-73053-3

First Minstrel Books printing June 1992

10 9 8 7 6 5 4 3 2 1

Printed in the U.S.A.

Contents

THE LEGEND OF
MINER'S CREEK

1

A Fiery Welcome

"What if lightning strikes the plane?" Bess Marvin said nervously. She leaned forward in the small aircraft and grabbed her friend Nancy Drew's arm as she spoke.

Nancy looked out the window at the black thunderhead clouds hovering just above and north of the light plane. From her seat next to the pilot, eighteen-year-old Nancy had a clear view of the gathering summer storm. Soon the clouds would block out the sun that filtered through the window and accented the red highlights in Nancy's blond hair. Below the clouds she saw the jagged peaks of Washington State's Cascade Mountains.

"I think we're safe for now," Nancy said. She leaned around the back of her seat so she could smile at Bess, who was directly behind her. Nancy was used to reassuring her friend, who was often a reluctant participant in Nancy's adventures as a detective.

Now, seeing Bess's pale face, Nancy felt a twinge of sympathy. Bess was so scared that she hadn't even bothered to brush back the lock of long blond hair that had fallen out of place and hung across her cheek. And Bess's eyes, Nancy noticed, had lost their usual sparkle.

"Your friend's right." Their pilot, Beau Dalton Eastham, glanced over his shoulder at Bess. He was a large man, tall and sturdily built. Dark hair covered the sides of his head, but the top was bald and shiny. His straw cowboy hat hung on a special hook on the back of his pilot's seat. "The storm is a doozy, all right, but it's still quite a ways to the north," he said. "We'll be on the ground before it gets here."

Bess gave a deep sigh but didn't relax her grip on the back of Nancy's seat. Her fingernails were white from pressing against the metal.

"Watch it, or you'll break those precious nails," George Fayne said lightly from her seat next to Bess. George was Bess's cousin and, like Bess, a loyal friend of Nancy. Unlike Bess, George was tall and athletic. Her short, curly, dark-brown hair was full of bounce and seemed to reflect her energetic personality. "I'm sure Mr. Eastham knows what he's doing," George told Bess.

"Call me B.D.," the pilot broke in. "And you really can relax. I've been flying from Seattle to Eagle Point for twenty years now, and I—" His

2

words were cut short as the plane seemed to drop out from under the girls. Nancy felt her stomach jump to her throat just as a flash of lightning outlined a jagged peak to the north.

"Ahhh!"

Nancy turned in the direction of the scream. George's mouth was still open, as though she'd just had her breath stolen away. She was sitting up very straight in her seat. A glance at Bess's face told Nancy that her friend was too scared to say anything.

"Air pockets," B.D. announced as he worked the controls confidently. "But don't worry. We're coming up on the airport now."

The plane bumped three more times, as though running over rocks in the sky, before settling into a smooth descent.

"None too soon for me," George said.

Nancy looked out her window at the single runway coming up beneath them. As the plane landed with a jolting thump, Nancy could see their hosts waiting by a dusty blue van near the airport's only hangar. One other small building stood next to the hangar. Probably an office, Nancy thought. There was no terminal building, no paved parking lot, no one except Charlie Griffin and his granddaughter, Rachel, waiting for the plane to arrive.

"This is definitely the smallest airport I've ever seen," George said.

"It serves our needs," B.D. said as he turned the plane in a small circle and steered toward Charlie and Rachel. "Private planes and a few small charters are all that ever come here."

Charlie waved as the plane taxied to a stop. His hair had turned a rich silver and the creases in his face had grown deeper since Nancy had last seen him back in River Heights. He had been in Nancy's hometown to visit with her grandparents, who had enjoyed vacations at Charlie's rustic resort, Highland Retreat. Now, even in his early seventies, Charlie looked athletic and capable.

Rachel, Charlie's granddaughter, stood next to him. She was a slender teenager with fine brown hair pulled straight back in a loose ponytail. Nancy knew from her father, Carson Drew, that Rachel had been living at the retreat since her parents had died several years earlier, but the two girls had never met.

"Rough trip?" Charlie asked the girls as he opened the plane door.

"I'll say," Bess volunteered. "I hope we're taking the train back."

"No extra charge for the roller coaster ride," B.D. joked as he and Charlie exchanged slaps on the back.

Each of the girls got a firm handshake from Charlie and a cheerful smile from Rachel as introductions were made.

"Am I glad to see you," Rachel said. "Most of our guests are families with small children. It's not very often we have other teenagers at the retreat."

"And we're looking forward to having you show

us around," Nancy said. "We want to see everything."

"Yes, after we rest," Bess said. "After that plane trip I'm too shaken up for sight-seeing."

"Are you too shaken up for lunch?" Charlie asked as he and B.D. helped carry the girls' bags to the van. "The retreat is about twenty minutes from here. I thought we'd grab a bite to eat in town before we drive out."

"Take them to Miner's Creek Saloon," B.D. suggested. "They've got the best burgers in the county."

"Food, I can handle," Bess said. "All that excitement's made me hungry."

Nancy and George laughed. Bess was nearly always ready to eat.

"I'm starved, too," Nancy said. "And we'll have a chance to hear more about the sale of the Highland Retreat over lunch."

It had been three weeks since Charlie had called Nancy's father, a prominent River Heights attorney, for legal advice about the sale of Charlie's land. During that phone call, Charlie had also invited Nancy and her friends to visit before the resort was sold.

As the girls climbed into the van, Charlie asked B.D., "We still on for cribbage Thursday night?"

"I'm counting on it," B.D. said, smiling at Charlie. "And it's your turn to provide the food."

"Right. See you at nine," Charlie called as he climbed behind the wheel of the van.

"That B.D. is quite a pilot," George said to Charlie as he drove away.

"He's the best, all right," Charlie said. "B.D. flies a lot of our guests in to the retreat. I probably wouldn't be in business without him and his airport."

"B.D. is a good friend, too," Rachel added. "He spends a lot of time up at the Highlands, hiking and stuff, not to mention all those cribbage games with Granddad."

Nancy tried to picture the rugged B.D. turning cards and moving pegs along a cribbage board. It was easier to imagine him outdoors. "He seems more like a mountain man than a cribbage player," Nancy said.

"Well, he's that, too," Rachel said. "B.D.'s a fisherman and also the unofficial Eagle County historian."

"I'm not surprised to hear that," George said. "He was telling us stories during our flight about the fur trappers who were the first white settlers here."

"Before the gold prospectors," Bess added.

"B.D. tells all our guests that story. It gets them in the mood for their vacation at the retreat," Rachel said with a laugh. "A lot of the guests pan for gold in Miner's Creek. Some of them like that more than the hiking and animal watching."

As they drove down the main street of Eagle Point, Nancy felt as though she had been transported back one hundred years. The town looked

6

like an old western village, even though it catered to tourists and was really quite modern. The sidewalks were made of wood, and the buildings looked as if they had appeared straight out of an old cowboy movie.

Charlie parked on the street in front of Miner's Creek Saloon and showed the girls inside. The dining room had dark wooden paneling, brass fixtures, and checked curtains on the front windows. They ordered lunch, and their small table was soon covered with oversize cheeseburgers and big plates of home-style french fries.

"I think Bess is in heaven," George joked.

"I am," Bess answered. "And I think I'm going to love Eagle Point. It's just getting here that I could do without."

The others laughed and quickly dug into their food. Soon Charlie was mopping up the last dab of ketchup from his plate with a fat french fry.

"You asked about the Highlands sale earlier," Charlie said, turning to Nancy. He frowned and looked down at the table. "I guess your father told you I'm selling the place to the government. The money will help me pay for Rachel's college education."

Nancy suspected from his tone that Charlie wasn't completely happy about selling his land. She couldn't blame him for that. It was the only home he had ever known. She glanced at Rachel and saw that she, too, looked unhappy.

"I want to be a marine biologist," Rachel told the

7

girls with the same hint of sadness in her voice that Nancy had detected in Charlie's. "I wish Granddad didn't have to sell his land, but there's just no other way."

"My Rachel will be able to do a lot of good for the environment," Charlie said. He reached across the table to touch his granddaughter's hand gently. "And we should have the money from the sale next year. . . . That is, if everything goes right."

"Sometimes I wonder if it's going to," Rachel said with a sigh. "So many things have happened on the retreat this summer."

"Like what?" Nancy asked quickly. She was well known around River Heights for solving cases that had baffled the police. Any hint of a mystery always got her attention.

"Oh, nothing serious," Charlie said. "Little things, like papers disappearing."

"Papers having to do with the sale?" Nancy asked.

"Yes," Rachel said, leaning forward. "You see, before the government can buy the land, the state legislature has to agree to pay for it. We're counting on Senator John P. Callihan, who used to live here in Eagle Point, to convince them to do that. He said he'd help, but the forms he sends Granddad keep disappearing."

"Lost in the mail," Charlie broke in lightly. "No mystery there. Just Rachel's overactive imagination, I'm afraid."

"Maybe, but what about the fires?" Rachel said,

looking squarely at her grandfather. "Even you can't explain those away so easily."

Charlie's smile was replaced by a frown. Nancy thought she saw a look of sadness in his eyes—or was it fear?

"Do you mean there have been fires at the Highlands?" Nancy asked.

"Just small ones," Charlie said, still frowning. "And I don't think they're much of a mystery either, really."

"Granddad thinks the fires have been accidentally set by guests," Rachel said. "Sometimes people are pretty careless with cigarettes and matches."

"Did you find cigarettes or matches at the fires?" Nancy asked.

Charlie shook his head. "No. Nothing," he said. "That is a little strange, I guess, but I wouldn't call it a mystery. Nothing like what you're used to, Nancy."

Nancy thought about their conversation as she and her friends followed Charlie and Rachel out of the restaurant. There was probably a logical explanation for the fires, she decided finally. As they pushed through the doors to the rustic main street, Nancy breathed in the pine-scented air and thought about how much she was going to enjoy her relaxing vacation.

After climbing into the van, Nancy, Bess, and George didn't have to wait long to get a firsthand view of the ancient Cascade forests. The paved road quickly gave way to dirt. On both sides of the road hundred-year-old evergreen trees stretched to the sky.

"This is our property on the right," Charlie said. "The U.S. Forest Service owns the land on the other side of the road."

"It's beautiful," Nancy said. "A fire here would be a real tragedy."

"It certainly would," Charlie agreed. "Fire could destroy the forest and our business at the same time. Fortunately, we've been able to avoid any major disasters so far."

Rachel pointed out the van window. "It looks as if we're in for a big storm."

Nancy followed Rachel's gaze. The trees along the road had been replaced by a large, grassy meadow. Beyond the meadow the mountains reached skyward, their snowcapped peaks hidden by heavy black clouds. The storm clouds that they had seen to the north from the airplane now completely covered the sky. Nancy heard a rumble of thunder in the distance.

"It sure does look like rain," George said.

"I hope so," Rachel said. "Sometimes the lightning comes without rain. That's when we worry most about fires."

"Can't you tell by looking if there's rain in the storm?" Bess asked.

"No, but sometimes I can smell the rain in the air. Then I know the forest is safe." As she spoke, Rachel rolled down her window. But instead of rain, Nancy caught the faint smell of burning grass.

10

So did Rachel. "I smell smoke, Granddad," she said.

"So do I," Charlie said grimly. He pulled the van to the side of the dirt road, and he and the girls climbed out. "We'd better find the source fast. The whole forest could go up."

He and the girls peered out into the meadow, looking for any sign of fire. The air was very still, and it was hard to tell which direction the smoke was coming from. Nancy wished she could see over the grass. She looked around for something to stand on. Just off the right side of the road, she spotted a round granite rock at least four feet tall. Nancy reached it with three long steps and scrambled on top. From her higher position she could see a small patch of burning grass. The flames were edging their way outward, as though the fire had not yet chosen a direction.

"There," Nancy said. "Three, maybe four hundred yards away."

The others looked in the direction Nancy pointed.

"I still don't see it," George said, squinting.

Just then a strong gust of wind whipped across the meadow. Orange flames shot skyward and spread quickly through the dry grass. Nancy knew there was no longer any question about which way the fire would go. It was moving quickly—straight toward the trees!

2

Racing the Wind

Nancy jumped from the rock and ran back toward her friends. Fortunately, Charlie and Rachel knew exactly what to do. Living in the forest had taught them to prepare for just this sort of emergency. Like many of their neighbors, they carried short-handled shovels and a bucket in their vehicle. It took Charlie only a moment to break out the fire-fighting equipment.

"Rachel, go get Pete!" Charlie yelled as he handed shovels to Nancy and George and took the last one for himself. "Take Bess with you and call the Forest Service. If we don't get this stopped before it reaches the trees, we've got big trouble."

Again, thunder rumbled in the distance. Nancy looked up at the clouds, remembering that they couldn't count on the storm for rain.

Dust billowed up from the van as Rachel and Bess

drove away. Charlie raced into the tall grass of the meadow, with George and Nancy close behind.

"Be careful of the creek!" Charlie shouted as Nancy came up beside him. "It's just ahead of you."

His cry was just in time to save Nancy from slipping into the deep water. The tall grass had hidden the creek bank from view.

Charlie ran downstream to shallower water and waded quickly across. Nancy and George followed him, barely caring that their shoes were soaked in the process. On the far bank Nancy could hear the crackle of the fire as the wind whipped it through the grass. She let Charlie stay in the lead as they raced alongside the fire, down the meadow. The wind was at their backs, pushing the flames through dried grass and wildflowers. Nancy realized they would have to outrun the blaze to stop it. Once out in front they could use their shovels to build a fire line of dirt that the flames could not cross—if they were lucky.

Nancy was surprised at how quickly the fire was moving. She ran her fastest through the uneven ground of the meadow. Charlie was still in front of her, his surefootedness making up for his age as they ran.

"Come on, we don't have much time," Charlie urged as he rounded the front edge of the fire. "Dig up the grass," he instructed the girls.

Nancy and George went to work, pushing their shovels into the dry earth and turning over the meadow grass.

13

Behind them the forest trees swayed in the wind. The huge evergreens that had stood undisturbed for more than a hundred years now depended entirely on Charlie, Nancy, and George for their safety.

"How'd this happen?" A new and demanding voice came from the direction of the woods. Nancy turned quickly to see a stocky, older woman behind her pitch in with the shoveling. The woman's short hair was a tousled mixture of brown and gray, and she wore a white T-shirt under blue striped overalls. Nancy had been so intent on throwing dirt that she hadn't seen the newcomer approach, carrying her own shovel.

"Maddie Emerson," Charlie called without missing a shovel beat. "Glad you showed up. We can use all the help we can get."

"I was on my way home. How'd this start?" the woman asked again.

"Don't know. Lightning, I guess," Charlie told her. Then with a few quick directions he split the group into pairs. He and George worked side by side, making a furrow two shovels wide through the meadow. Nancy and Maddie moved side by side in the opposite direction. By the time they had dug a line fifty feet long, Nancy was near exhaustion. The fire was drawing closer. The smoke was so thick, Nancy couldn't see Charlie and George at the other end of the fire line. Nancy's back was aching from the hard work, but she knew she couldn't stop digging.

Suddenly Maddie grabbed her roughly by the arm and jerked her aside. Nancy took two flying steps and fell sprawling into the meadow, just as the fire rushed through the grass behind her and stopped at the line of dirt they had just dug.

"Got no sense, young lady?" Maddie said gruffly. "You must be one of those city folks. Don't know when to get out from in front of a fire."

"I was trying to finish the line," Nancy said, scrambling to her feet. She was close enough to see the lines in the older woman's leathery skin.

"Well, it's as done as it's going to get," Maddie told her. She spoke quietly as she turned to watch the blaze, and the harshness had left her voice. "Now it will either hold or it won't."

Nancy watched as the flames gathered themselves behind the line. The fire appeared to be growing smaller as it ran out of grass to burn. Suddenly, with a mighty roar, the wind picked up again, whisking tongues of flame across the hard-dug trail of dirt. Once again the fire raced toward the forest, burning to the edge of the line of trees. Nancy and the others stood helpless as the first giant pine exploded into flames.

A flash of lightning and a crash of thunder seemed to announce their defeat. Nancy raised her head toward the sky. She could see why this kind of storm put the forest in so much danger. The huge thundercloud seemed to hang just overhead, ready to throw its lightning bolts toward the ground.

Another flash drew Nancy's eyes toward the mountains. There, rushing across the meadow, was a curtain of rain, blowing in with the wind! "Look!" Nancy cried, pointing toward the rain. Maddie saw it and breathed a heavy sigh of relief.

In another moment the downpour reached them. Nancy and Maddie were instantly drenched, and the fire that had seemed unstoppable minutes earlier was reduced to a few smoldering ashes. The danger was past.

Maddie and Nancy ran for the cover of the forest to wait for the storm to pass. Nancy could see Charlie and George coming toward them through the smoke. Their wet clothes clung to their bodies, and streams of water had turned the soot and dirt to mud on their faces. Despite their frazzled looks, both Charlie and George were smiling.

"That was close," George said. "I thought we'd lost the whole forest."

"I want to thank you girls for your help, and you, too, Maddie," Charlie said.

"You can thank people all you want, but sooner or later that's not going to be good enough," Maddie said. Her scowl had returned. "Looks to me like your luck is running out, Charlie Griffin."

"What do you mean by that?" Nancy asked, frowning.

"I mean, he'd better figure out a way to stop all of these fires, or Highland Retreat is going to be nothing but ashes."

"Now, Maddie, this could have been caused by

16

lightning," Charlie said. "Besides, it's under control."

"This time it is. But next time you may not be so lucky," Maddie said. Then she turned and started heading back toward her jeep.

"That almost sounded like some kind of threat," George said as Maddie waded across the creek and headed for the road.

"Oh, she's just mad about the sale," Charlie said. "Maddie runs a wild bird hospital. She cares for birds that have been shot or hit by cars. Maddie thinks a state park will bring more people and more problems for the birds."

The thundershower passed over in a matter of minutes, and Nancy, George and Charlie emerged from the forest. As Maddie drove away in her gray jeep, the retreat's van suddenly came into view. It parked by the big rock, and Rachel and Bess jumped out. Behind them was a dark-haired, stocky man. The three of them trudged through the wet grass as Nancy and George helped Charlie put out the embers from the fire.

"I guess you girls got an unusual welcome to Highland Retreat," the man said when they came up. He was of medium height, with broad shoulders and a large stomach that partially covered the big buckle on his western belt. His wide-brimmed brown cowboy hat kept the last drops of rain off his tanned face.

"This is Pete Sims, our main hand at the retreat," Rachel said.

17

"Pleased to meet you," Nancy said. "And our first day *has* been a little more exciting than we'd expected."

"And we haven't even gotten to our cabin yet," George added.

"You all run along now. I'll finish up," Pete said, waving toward the van.

Nancy thought fast. She wasn't ready to leave the fire scene quite yet. The first shadow of a doubt about the cause of this fire was forming in the back of her mind. Charlie had said it was probably the result of lightning, but Nancy remembered seeing lightning only near the mountains before the fire started. That, plus the fact that this wasn't the first suspicious fire on the retreat, made Nancy want to investigate.

"I'll catch up," she said to the others. "I think I lost my watch while I was digging." As she spoke, she quickly slipped her watch off her wrist and into her pocket.

"We'll help you look for it," Bess offered.

Nancy waved her friend away. "That's okay," she said. "I think I know exactly where it is."

As the others headed toward the van, Nancy began to follow the fire line, looking at the ground carefully as if searching for the watch. When she got to the end of the fire line, she circled around toward the spot where the fire had started. Pete was still back near the fire line, throwing dirt on the last embers. She hoped he wouldn't look up. Across the

18

meadow Charlie and the girls were almost to the van.

Nancy was looking for anything that seemed out of place—anything that would tell her someone had been near the start of the fire. She found nothing on the ground, but then, just as she was about to give up, she spotted a flash of white caught in the thorns of a low bush. Nancy reached in carefully and pulled out a partly burned piece of paper.

Suddenly she heard a noise behind her. Nancy turned to see Pete Sims scowling at her from beneath his wide hat brim.

"What do you have there?" he demanded.

3

Half a Clue

Nancy quickly tucked the paper into her pocket and pulled out her watch. "I found my watch," she said, showing it to Pete.

"Then you'd better get out of here," the dark-haired man ordered. "Don't you know this is a dangerous place to be? This fire could start up again any minute."

"Are you coming, too?" Nancy asked. She thought Pete seemed awfully anxious to be alone in the meadow.

"Soon enough," Pete told her shortly. "Now, go on before the van takes off without you." He gestured in the direction of the road, where Charlie and the girls had just reached the van.

"Sorry. Thanks for your help." Nancy tried to sound cheerful as she started off to join the others.

A few rays of sun streaked through the heavy clouds overhead. Bess stood by the van with her head hung to one side, squeezing the excess water out of her long blond hair. Her blue shorts and denim blouse were soaked to her skin. George and Rachel were already inside the van. They looked as if they had just been pushed into a swimming pool with their clothes on. Everyone was smudged with dirt and ash. They could all use warm showers, Nancy thought.

"How will Pete get back?" she asked as Charlie held open the van door for her.

"Don't worry," Rachel volunteered. "There's a trail that leads from the meadow back to the lodge. In fact, Pete was just coming back from there when we found him and told him about the fire."

"He'd been in the meadow?" Nancy asked in surprise.

Rachel nodded. "He'd been putting out a salt block to attract deer for the guests to watch." She paused, frowning. "He seemed very surprised about the fire. He hadn't noticed it when he was there, so it must have just started," she said.

It seemed to Nancy that a lot of people had "happened" to be around the fire scene. Pete had been in the meadow just before it started. Maddie Emerson had shown up just after. It was even an interesting coincidence, she thought, that the fire had started as they were driving by. Could someone have planned for them to see it? She remembered Maddie's words: "He'd better figure out a way to stop all of these fires, or Highland Retreat is going to be ashes."

21

Could Maddie Emerson have been threatening Charlie instead of warning him?

Nancy reached into the pocket of her shorts and carefully pulled out the soggy paper that she had found in the bush.

"What's that?" George asked.

"I'm not sure," Nancy said. She looked at the note briefly, but she could make out nothing of what was left of the words.

"Did you drop this?" she asked Charlie, handing the note over the seat to him.

The van slowed as Charlie looked at the paper and handed it back. "Never seen it," he said. "Where did it come from?"

"It was near the fire," Nancy answered. She spread the paper out on her lap and once again tried to decipher the words.

> *ly 13, 19*
> *say Labo*
> *n Home Rd.*
> *eport*
> *mple #653*
> *and Re*

The rest of the message had been smudged or burned away.

"I can't tell anything from that," Bess said from her seat beside Nancy.

"The first line must be the date," Nancy said.

"That's the day before yesterday. Whoever received this letter must have gotten it within the last two days—and he or she could have dropped it in the meadow right before the fire."

"Do you think someone started the fire?" George asked.

"Maybe," Nancy said. "But if so, who? And why would anyone want to do something like that?"

"Now, wait a minute," Charlie broke in, glancing in the rearview mirror. "I think you girls are getting carried away with all this mystery stuff," he said. "The fire was started by lightning. There's no mystery in that."

"Your grandfather's probably right," Nancy said to Rachel, tucking the paper back in her pocket. "You said yourself the storm could be dangerous."

Rachel looked unconvinced, but she didn't say anything more as the van rounded the turn into the retreat. On the left stood a large barn with horse corrals behind it. Across the road from the barn Rachel pointed out Pete's small house and a row of five cabins with a creek flowing behind them. At the end of the row of cabins a large wooden lodge perched on a hill at a bend in the creek.

Charlie stopped in front of the cabin closest to the lodge just as a truck with a United States Forest Service emblem on the side drove up the driveway behind them. It was a small fire-fighting truck, with a water tank and hoses on the sides.

"You girls have an hour to clean up before

dinner," Charlie said, unlocking the cabin door. "Rachel and I'll go talk to the men in green—and tell them they're late."

Nancy, Bess, and George threw their suitcases on the two sets of bunk beds and began to peel off their rain-soaked shoes and socks. The cabin was rustic but comfortable. One room served as both living room and bedroom. Off that room was a small kitchen and a counter with four chairs. There was also a small bathroom with a shower, which the girls took turns using to scrub off the mud and ashes.

"I feel a hundred percent better," Bess said as she straightened the collar of her mint-green shirt. "Next time let's leave the fire fighting to the Forest Service."

"Let's hope there isn't a next time," Nancy said. "That fire could have been disastrous."

"You don't think it was caused by lightning, do you?" George asked, lacing up a pair of clean white tennis shoes.

"I'm not sure," Nancy said. She explained why she'd thought that the fire had started before the lightning arrived. "It could have been arson," she said. "But why would someone want to burn down a beautiful forest?"

"To scare tourists away?" George suggested.

"We know Maddie would like to do that," Nancy said. "But she wouldn't want to destroy the trees."

"And Maddie helped put the fire out," George

added. "Why would she do that if she had started it in the first place?"

"So we wouldn't suspect her?" Bess suggested. She was standing in front of a small mirror, brushing her hair as she spoke. "Maybe Maddie was afraid someone had seen her too close to the fire, and she wanted to protect herself."

"I think Maddie's definitely a suspect," Nancy said. "But she's not the only one."

"That's right. Pete was there, too," Bess said. "And he was awfully anxious to get us out of there."

"We need more information," Nancy said as the three of them closed their suitcases and started toward the lodge for dinner. "Let's keep our eyes and ears open tonight and see if we can learn more."

The rainstorm had settled the dust on the retreat's dirt driveway, and a fresh mountain scent mingled pleasantly with the faint smell of food as the girls neared the lodge. Nancy rapped on the big wooden screen door, and the girls were quickly greeted by a motherly looking woman in a ruffled apron.

"Come right in. Guests don't need to knock," she said, smiling broadly. "You must be Nancy, George, and Bess. I'm Elsa Parker, the cook. Dinner's almost ready."

"I can't wait," Bess said. "Can we help?"

"Thank you, but it's all under control," Elsa said. "In fact, I believe Rachel is just finishing the salad. I'll send her out."

While they waited for Rachel, the girls looked around the main room of the lodge. They had entered beneath a balcony that overlooked the main floor. A huge stone fireplace covered most of the far wall of the room, with the rock work climbing two stories high. In front of the fireplace a large wooden table was set for dinner. Several of the retreat's other guests were already gathered nearby.

"Let's go over and meet people," George suggested, but Nancy had already spotted a large display of old pictures and mining equipment arranged on the wall beneath the balcony.

"I'd like to check this out first," she said, nodding toward the shelves and glass cases of old artifacts.

Bess was quickly attracted by a small piece of snowy-white quartz with gold-colored veins running through it. It was displayed on a shelf inside a locked case beneath a small miner's pick.

"Pretty, isn't it?" Rachel said, surprising the girls as she entered the room. "It's valuable, too."

"It's really gold, then?" Bess asked.

"Yes, running through the quartz," Rachel said. "Wait here a minute." She disappeared into the kitchen and came back with a small gold key. After unlocking the case, she picked up the piece of quartz and handed it to Bess. "For such a small rock it's pretty heavy, isn't it?"

"I'll say," George said, taking the quartz from Bess. She passed it on to Nancy.

26

"Gold is one of the heaviest metals," Rachel explained. "That's why it settled to the bottom of the prospectors' pans." Rachel took the gold ore from Nancy and set it on a nearby shelf before pointing to a deep pan with sloping sides that sat on a special stand. "That's what the prospectors used to pan for gold."

"It looks a little like a wok," George commented.

"It's shaped for washing sand," Rachel said, picking up the pan. "People use the same 'panning' technique today. They swirl a pan full of sand around with water until all but the heaviest material washes away. What's left is usually black sand. With luck there will be gold flakes or nuggets in with it."

The girls could see black sand in the bottom of the display pan, but there was no gold in it.

"Is the sand valuable?" George asked.

"No, it's just for show," Rachel told her, putting the pan back in place.

"But the white quartz is worth something, I bet," Bess said.

"Yes, but it's important to Granddad and me because of its history," Rachel explained.

"Where did it come from?" Nancy asked.

"Charlie got it from his dad, Cyrus," Rachel explained. "It was found near Miner's Creek by a prospector named Jeremiah Benner. He was using that pickax right there above the quartz. But Charlie tells the story better than I do."

"Dinner's ready!" Elsa's voice echoed through the big lodge as she placed a large bowl of potatoes on the table.

"And I'm ready for dinner," Bess said as she and George followed Rachel to the table.

Nancy was about to follow when she heard the sound of an argument on the porch outside.

"I told you everything is fine," a voice said.

Nancy could tell that the speaker was Charlie, but he sounded very nervous. She didn't recognize the second voice.

"You don't seem to understand how serious this matter is," the second man said sternly. "The senator isn't going to be pleased. Any more problems and the park deal is off!"

28

4

Jeremiah's Gold

Nancy edged her way toward the front door of the lodge, pretending to be interested in a picture on the wall. She was hoping to get a glimpse, through the screen door, of the stranger on the porch. Unfortunately, Charlie spotted her. There was an awkward moment of silence as Charlie realized his conversation had been overheard.

"Excuse me, but dinner is ready," Nancy said quickly.

"Thank you, Nancy," Charlie said, looking somewhat relieved. He pushed the screen door open and introduced Nancy to a handsome young man in a well-tailored suit. "Nancy Drew, this is Tyler Nelson," Charlie said.

The young man forced a tense smile and extended his hand to Nancy.

"Nancy helped us fight the fire today," Charlie told Tyler as the man and Nancy shook hands.

"Charlie thinks the fire was started by lightning," Tyler said. He studied Nancy, as though waiting to see if she would contradict Charlie's story.

"We were lucky the rain put it out," Nancy answered, trying to avoid saying anything definite.

"We can all be glad of that," Tyler said, looking at Nancy with piercing blue eyes. "Senator Callihan is beginning to think this place is too dangerous for a park."

"Tyler, here, is an aide for the senator," Charlie explained.

"Yes, I just flew in tonight to check some records and take a few pictures," Tyler said.

"And get some dinner, I hope," Charlie said. He seemed anxious to end the awkward meeting. "Let's eat." He led the way in to the table before either Nancy or Tyler could say anything else.

At the table Charlie introduced the girls to the other guests.

"Shirley and Frank Kauffman and their son, Aaron, have the first cabin," Charlie said, gesturing to a family at the end of the table. The man and woman both wore bright flannel shirts and blue jeans. The man was tall and blond. His wife had long black hair fastened with a barrette. "They've come here every year since Aaron was born," Charlie went on. "That's five years, isn't it?"

Both the Kauffmans nodded, looking pleased that Charlie remembered their son's age. Shirley gently pushed a stray strand of black hair from her son's eyes. Aaron was swinging his feet vigorously under the table. A boy with lots of energy, Nancy guessed.

"And this is Todd and Beth Smythe, who are here for their honeymoon. They're in the middle cabin," Charlie said.

The newlyweds held hands and smiled at each other as they were introduced. Both had dressed up for dinner—Todd in a checked cotton shirt with a narrow western tie, and Beth in a ruffled blouse and long skirt.

Pete and Elsa sat at the table with the guests, as did Tyler Nelson. Pete had changed into a plaid shirt that stretched a little too tightly across his chest, straining the fabric. He was the first to dig into the potatoes, Nancy noticed.

The platters of food were soon empty, much to Elsa's delight. Bess was working on her second helping of steak.

"I'm so glad you liked the venison," Elsa said, beaming. "Some people don't, you know."

Bess stopped chewing and pushed aside the last bites on her plate.

"This is deer meat?" she asked weakly.

"Yes," Charlie said. "And Elsa fixes it better than anyone I know."

"Don't listen to him," Elsa said as she began to clear the dishes. "He's just trying to butter me up so he'll get a bigger piece of dessert."

"I'll help Elsa while you tell everyone the story of Jeremiah Benner," Rachel said to Charlie as she jumped to her feet. "It'll get them in the mood for a ride to Prospector's Canyon."

"We'd love to hear it," Nancy said eagerly.

Charlie pushed his chair back from the table. "This is the legend of Miner's Creek," he began. "And it all begins with a man named Jeremiah Benner.

"Jeremiah was a prospector in these parts. No one seems to know where he came from, or where he finally went, but while he was here, about seventy years ago, he was supposed to have found one of the county's richest gold mines."

Nancy looked around the table. She could see that Charlie had caught all of his guests' attention with the mention of gold, including Tyler Nelson.

"He panned a lot of gold out of Miner's Creek," Charlie went on. "Jeremiah was convinced that the mother lode—the source of all the gold—was someplace on this property. He was so convinced, in fact, that he agreed to make my father, Cyrus, his partner. Jeremiah said he'd give him half of whatever he found. In exchange, my father let him continue to prospect on this land.

"Jeremiah looked for all of one summer and most of the next. Then one evening, just before dark, he came running down the trail from Prospector's Canyon, his old burro hurrying along behind, pots and pans banging as they ran. He was shouting, 'I'm rich! I'm rich! I struck it rich!'"

Charlie paused for a moment. Elsa and Rachel

32

were busy setting plates of German chocolate cake in front of each guest.

"What Jeremiah had found were two pieces of quartz with gold in them," Charlie continued. "He kept one for himself and gave the other to Cyrus. He said he'd found a pocket of that quartz ore that was so heavy with gold he'd only be able to carry a little of it out at a time. But he refused to tell Cyrus where it was. Cyrus never got anything more after that one piece of quartz, which most of you have seen on that shelf over by the door."

"But what happened to Jeremiah?" George asked.

Charlie shook his head. "No one knows. He sneaked around in and out of the mountains for about a month after that. Then he just disappeared. According to my father, his burro wandered into the barn one day with its halter still on, looking for food. But no one ever saw Jeremiah again."

"Now, *that's* a mystery," George whispered to Nancy.

"My dad, Cyrus, died of smallpox shortly after that, leaving Ma and me alone. I don't remember anything about Jeremiah, except from stories." Charlie leaned back in his chair.

There was silence around the table for a moment.

"I never even knew there was gold in Washington State," Bess said at last.

"Yes, we have the same mountain formation as California and Alaska," Rachel explained. She had finished serving cake and was once again sitting at the table next to Nancy. "Of course, there haven't been as many stories about Washington, but we've had our share of prospectors. Some of them got rich, just like they did in California."

"Did you look for the gold yourself?" Nancy asked Charlie as she finished her cake.

The old man shrugged. "I did, some, but I never found anything. Neither did any of the other people who came looking," Charlie said. "My guess is that Jeremiah found these two pieces of quartz and that was all. I don't think there ever was a mine. Jeremiah, once he figured that out, probably headed for Alaska, hoping to strike gold there."

"Now I can't wait to see Prospector's Canyon," Mrs. Kauffman said.

"Maybe we can find gold," Aaron added eagerly. He looked down the table at Charlie, his eyes wide with excitement.

"We'll ride horses to the canyon day after tomorrow," Rachel promised.

Everyone agreed that they'd like to see the place where Jeremiah supposedly struck it rich.

"It sounds like a tall tale to me," Tyler said. He held his water glass casually in one hand as he spoke. Still wearing a suit, he looked out of place in the rustic surroundings, Nancy thought.

"Oh, but the ride will be fun," Bess said.

"Well, I say you're off on a wild-goose chase," Tyler continued. "And Charlie told me the best scenery is north of the meadow. Why don't you take your ride there?"

"Maybe we'll go both places," Rachel said.

Tyler folded his napkin and, after thanking his hosts, excused himself from the table. "I've got some reading to do. Good night, everyone," he said abruptly, then walked out the front door of the lodge.

"What's *his* problem?" Bess said under her breath.

"If I didn't know better, I'd think he wanted us all to stay away from Prospector's Canyon," George whispered to Nancy.

"Which makes me all the more determined to go," Nancy said. "This has been a very interesting day."

Nancy, Bess, and George helped Elsa and Rachel carry dishes into the kitchen. The other guests slowly returned to their own cabins.

When the table was cleared, Elsa brought mugs and a pot of tea. Charlie lit a small fire in the fireplace, and the girls pulled chairs in a half circle around it.

"Is the sale really in danger of falling through?" Nancy asked Charlie.

Charlie sighed. "According to Tyler it is. He says Senator Callihan doesn't like the reports of problems here. Money is tight right now, and he's having trouble getting the votes to buy the place."

"Someone could be trying to stop the sale,"

Nancy said gently. "I'm still not convinced that fire today was caused by lightning."

"It could have been lightning, but I have to admit, the timing seemed wrong," Charlie said slowly. He took a sip of tea. "But who would do such a thing?"

"Maddie, for one," George volunteered.

"Or Pete," Bess added. "Neither of them were very nice today at the fire."

"Nonsense," Charlie said without hesitation. "Maddie loves the land in these parts more than anyone I know, and Pete has lived here for twenty years. He wouldn't try to burn his own home."

"If the Highlands becomes a state park, will Pete have to move?" Nancy asked carefully.

Charlie was silent for a moment. "Yes," he answered quietly. "According to the agreement, I can live here for the rest of my life, but Pete would have to be out by the end of the year. But I could never believe that Pete would start that fire."

"What would you do if the state didn't buy the land?" Nancy asked. "Couldn't you sell to someone else?"

Charlie nodded. "There is a second offer, but I'd feel better about selling the land if it was going to be a park. Then I could be sure it would be taken care of," he said.

"Who made you the second offer?" Nancy asked.

"I'll show you the letter," Charlie said, rising from his chair. He crossed the room to a large rolltop desk under the staircase that led to the balcony. Then he pulled a letter from the top drawer and handed it to Nancy.

At the top of the letter were three eagles, above an address for the Nature Preservation League. The eagles looked to Nancy as if they had been printed by a computer. The letter read:

Dear Mr. Griffin:

It has come to our attention that the Highland Retreat may be for sale. We are very interested in buying and preserving land in your area. Though we could not offer as much as some, you could rest assured that your land would be in good hands. Please contact us at the above address.

> Sincerely,
> Rosco Johnson

"May I take the letter?" Nancy asked. "I'd like to check out this Nature Preservation League."

"What are you checking for?" Bess asked.

"I'm not sure," Nancy said. "But if this group is so anxious to buy the land, they might have a reason to try to stop the government deal. I think it's worth looking into."

With Charlie's permission Nancy took the letter, and the girls started to leave for their cabin. Rachel and Charlie walked them to the door of the lodge.

Suddenly Rachel gasped as they passed the display of mining equipment.

"The gold quartz!" she cried. "It's gone!"

5

In Harm's Way

Everyone whirled around to look at the shelf where the quartz had been.

"I left it out," Rachel blurted. "I remember, I took it from the locked case and left it here." She pointed to the shelf where she had placed the rock while explaining to the girls how to pan for gold. There were only a few books on it.

"Maybe it got knocked down or put in the wrong place," Bess suggested. She and Rachel began to look around on the floor and the other shelves, but they didn't find anything.

"Who could have taken it?" George asked, frowning.

"Anyone who was at dinner," Nancy said. "All of the guests walked by here on their way out. Any one of them could have picked up the quartz."

"But why?" Rachel shrugged her shoulders in confusion.

Nancy turned to Charlie. For the first time that

day he really did look like an old man. The lines in his face seemed deeper, and his eyes looked sad and tired.

"I'm beginning to think you and Rachel are right, Nancy," he said slowly. "There are just too many things going wrong—the fires, the quartz, the difficulty with the sale of our land. It's as though someone is trying to take everything that matters away from us."

Nancy took a deep breath. "I'm afraid I have to agree with you," she said. "I'm so sorry about your gold ore. Let's try and figure out who is behind these problems—and why. I'd like to take a trip back to the meadow to check out the fire site more thoroughly."

"I'll take you right after breakfast," Rachel volunteered.

The girls said good night to Rachel and Charlie and walked to their cabin.

"I hope the beds are comfortable," Bess said as they opened the door.

"After a day like this, I think I could sleep on anything," George said.

Nancy agreed, but once she was in her top bunk, she found her head swimming with the events of the day. It was at least an hour before she finally got to sleep.

"Rise and shine!" Rachel announced cheerfully as she pounded on the girls' cabin door the next morning. "Breakfast in thirty minutes."

Breakfast turned out to be homemade blueberry muffins, crisp bacon, scrambled eggs, juice, and hot cocoa served buffet-style in the lodge.

Nancy, George, and Bess had the spread all to themselves.

"Charlie's in his office doing paperwork, and the Kauffmans have already eaten," Rachel told them. "Apparently Aaron woke his parents early this morning," she added with a laugh. "The honeymooners are still asleep. We usually let guests sleep as late as they want, but I'm anxious to get started solving this mystery."

"Don't you mean *mysteries?*" George asked. "It seems to me there's more than one here."

"That's right," Bess agreed. "There's the mystery of the fires and of someone trying to stop the sale of your grandfather's land. And then there's the mystery of the stolen gold ore."

"That's my fault," Rachel said, looking at the floor. "I shouldn't have left the quartz out where it could be stolen."

Nancy wanted to tell Rachel everything would be all right, but so far the mysteries were baffling even to her.

After breakfast the girls followed Rachel out of the lodge. They waved to the Kauffmans, who were walking toward their car. Little Aaron was several paces behind his parents, examining a rock near the road.

"I think it's gold!" Aaron cried out, holding up the rock.

Bess laughed as his parents pretended to be very excited about his find.

"It looks like Aaron's caught gold fever," Rachel said with a laugh.

She led the girls along a path to the meadow, her long legs striding quickly. They crossed Miner's Creek, using a small footbridge suspended by ropes from four large pine trees. Bess was reluctant to cross the wobbly bridge but finally decided it was better than getting her feet wet by wading.

The trail wound through grass and wildflowers. The storm had blown over, leaving behind a brilliant blue sky. Beyond the meadow the snowcapped mountains finished a postcard-perfect setting.

They passed the salt lick that Pete had set out the day before. Rachel showed the girls deer tracks around the block, but there were no animals in sight.

"Over here," Nancy said when they neared the fire site. "I can see the ashes."

She led them off the trail to the place where the fire had started. She was standing at the point of a triangle of burned grass that had its longest edge at the line of trees where the meadow ended.

"The wind blew the fire in that direction," Nancy said, pointing to the trees. "So it had to have started here."

She led the way along the burned edge of grass, looking for clues as she went. Near the trees Nancy found tracks where the meadow grass had been crushed by the tires of a large vehicle.

"Is there a road close to here?" Nancy asked Rachel.

"There are old logging roads all through the woods," Rachel replied. "But I don't know why anyone would be driving in the meadow."

"Unless they were here to start a fire," Nancy said.

Nancy followed the tire tracks to the edge of the trees, but then they disappeared in the deep bed of pine needles. A jeep or truck could have easily maneuvered between the trees and back to the dirt road leading to town.

"The only thing all these tracks really tell us is that someone has been here within the last few days," Nancy said. "We're at a dead end, I'm afraid. Our best clue still seems to be the piece of paper I found in the bush. We know for sure that it was dropped recently—maybe by the person who drove whatever vehicle made these tracks."

The girls walked back along the trail toward the footbridge. When they reached the creek, Rachel made a sudden startled jump straight into the air.

"A water snake," Rachel told the others with a sheepish laugh. "They're harmless, but they always make me jump."

"A snake!" Bess sounded shocked. "Are there more?"

"Sure," Rachel answered.

"Are any of them dangerous?" Bess formed her words slowly.

"There are some rattlesnakes," Rachel said with a shrug. "But they mostly stay hidden during the heat of the day."

Bess nodded, glancing nervously at the ground.

"There are so many different animals in the Highlands, and I love them all," Rachel went on. "That's why I want to be a marine biologist some-day, so I can help wildlife and the environment."

"Why a *marine* biologist?" Nancy asked.

"Mostly because of the salmon," Rachel replied. "Every fall I watch them swim up Miner's Creek to spawn. And every spring the baby salmon swim hundreds of miles back to the ocean. I've always wanted to follow them to see where they live the rest of their lives. Come on, I'll show you my special place."

Instead of crossing the footbridge, Rachel led the girls along the creek to a salmon spawning bed she had restored in a straight stretch of clear, shallow water.

"This is it," Rachel said proudly. "I hauled in that round gravel on the bottom of the creek myself. The salmon bury their eggs in it."

To Nancy, the bed had seemed unimpressive at first—just a wide stretch of rapidly flowing water —but Rachel's explanation made it much more interesting.

"The real work was over here," Rachel continued. Nancy, Bess, and George followed her to a dam of rocks and concrete built at the entrance to a narrow ravine. Behind the dam was a pool of muddy water.

"This fills up every time it rains," Rachel said. "Without the dam the floodwater from that ravine would run into the stream. Then mud would smother the eggs and ruin the spawning bed."

"That must have been a lot of work," Bess said, looking at the four-foot-high dam.

Rachel nodded. "It sure was. It took me most of the summer to build," she explained. "Luckily, there are a lot of rocks around here, but I still had to carry all the concrete and roll the rocks into place. Thank goodness I had Maddie to help."

"Maddie Emerson?" Nancy wasn't surprised that the two were friends. Rachel had been quick to defend Maddie after the fire the day before.

"That's right," Rachel said. "Maddie knows a lot about most of the animals that live around here, not just birds."

As Rachel took the girls on a shortcut back to the lodge, Nancy hoped silently that Maddie wasn't involved in the problems at the retreat. It would be hard for Rachel to learn that she had been betrayed by someone who shared her love of nature.

"We can cross on this log," Rachel said, leading them to a fallen tree that made a natural bridge across the stream. What was left of the tree's large branches provided good handholds, and the girls made the crossing easily.

The four of them climbed the bank toward the lodge. As they headed through the trees, Nancy heard the sound of a jeep. Briefly she wondered whether Charlie had gone into town and was returning home.

It wasn't until they had stepped out of the trees that Nancy saw an old army jeep just a few yards away. It was headed straight toward them—and there was no one at the wheel!

6

Friends and Neighbors

Quickly Nancy grabbed Rachel and pulled her out of the way of the runaway jeep. George and Bess jumped to safety just in time and rolled into the pine needles under the trees.

"Phew! That was close," George said as she and Bess got up and brushed themselves off.

Then Rachel gasped. "The gas truck!" she cried, pointing in the direction of the lodge.

Nancy saw a small tank truck parked next to the retreat's gas pump beside the lodge. The truck was apparently making a delivery.

"The jeep's heading straight for it!" George yelled.

Without hesitation Nancy ran after the jeep. If it collided with the gasoline tanker, there could be a gas spill into Miner's Creek—or, even worse, an explosion.

"Stay back!" Nancy called over her shoulder. She

wasn't at all sure she could stop the jeep in time, and an explosion would almost certainly destroy the lodge.

Bounding over the uneven ground, she finally reached the door handle and wrenched it open. The truck was directly ahead. The deliveryman had just come around from behind his tanker and realized the danger. He waved his arms frantically at Nancy.

With her left hand on the open door, Nancy took a mighty leap and grabbed for the steering wheel, landing in the driver's seat. She immediately saw that a board was holding down the gas pedal. The steering wheel was also tied in place, forcing the jeep to hold to its collision course. Nancy kicked the board away with her foot, then stomped on the brake, hard. The jeep stopped with a lurch, just inches from the tank truck. Nancy shakily turned off the ignition, and the engine went silent.

The deliveryman came running through the dust that the jeep had kicked up. "That was some rescue," he said, obviously impressed.

Rachel, Bess, and George had also run to the jeep. Todd and Beth Smythe, who had seen all the action as they walked to the lodge, came up from the opposite direction. Nancy found herself surrounded by an admiring group.

"I bet you could be a movie stuntwoman," Todd Smythe said.

"You certainly saved my tanker," the deliveryman said. "And probably saved the lodge as well."

"Thanks," Nancy said, feeling her face grow red from all of the attention. "But you would have done the same thing if you'd had the chance. Do you deliver here often?"

"The first Tuesday of every month," the man answered, wiping his forehead with a handkerchief. "But I've never had a close call like this."

Nancy excused herself and started to follow the tracks left by the jeep. Clearly, someone had planned the near-disaster, and she was determined to find out who.

"Do you think that jeep was aimed at the gas truck or at us?" Bess asked, taking several running steps to keep up with Nancy's long strides.

Nancy frowned. "I'm not sure. But either way it took careful timing. Rachel, do you know whose jeep this is?"

"It belongs to the retreat," Rachel answered.

"Let's hurry and see if we can catch whoever did this," Nancy said.

George, Bess, and Rachel hurried after Nancy as she backtracked in the direction the jeep had come. Nancy realized that, by putting the jeep in low gear, whoever started it had given himself or herself time to get away from the scene. Even so, the person couldn't have gone far.

"Where is that jeep usually parked?" Nancy asked.

"Beside the barn," Rachel answered.

"It looks as if that's where these tracks lead,"

Nancy said. When she reached the jeep's usual parking spot, she turned and looked toward the lodge. It was a straight shot across an open area.

"Whoever was responsible could have done all his work right here, then started the engine and disappeared behind the barn," Nancy said. "Let's take a look."

As they neared the back corner of the barn, Nancy raised her finger to her lips, signaling the others to be quiet. There were voices coming from inside the barn.

Nancy leaned close to the door, but she couldn't make out what was being said.

"This way," Rachel whispered. She motioned to Nancy to follow her to a ladder that led to a hayloft in the top of the barn.

"We'll be able to hear from up there," Rachel said.

George and Bess offered to stay below as lookouts, and Nancy and Rachel climbed carefully up the old ladder.

The loft was one open room, half full of hay bales. Spaced along each side were openings in the floor, through which hay could be thrown down to each horse stall. Nancy and Rachel flattened themselves on their stomachs near one of the holes.

Below, Maddie and Pete were talking in angry voices. Nancy could hear clearly what was being said.

"It's not right that they should kick me out of my

home," Pete grumbled. "I've worked here for twenty years. It's not going to be easy to find another place to live, or another job."

"I don't blame you for being angry about the sale," Maddie said. "And the last thing *I* want is crowds of city folks stomping through the woods."

"Well, if it keeps burning, we may not have to worry about that," Pete said.

"That would be—"

Suddenly Nancy heard a creak, like that of a door hinge. Maddie stopped in midsentence. She and Pete both looked toward the barn door.

Pete strode to the door and yanked it open. Bess and George came tumbling into the barn.

"I can explain," Bess said quickly. "We were looking for lunch."

"She means horses," George corrected, but it was easy to see that Pete wasn't buying the story. He pushed his hat back, revealing the grim expression on his face.

"I think you two were snooping around," Pete accused, folding his arms across his chest. "And I want to know why."

The cousins looked at each other, as if both of them were waiting for the other to answer. Then the two of them looked at the floor, speechless.

Quickly Nancy climbed down the ladder from the loft and jumped to the floor behind Pete. Rachel was right behind her. Pete whirled around in surprise.

"I'll tell you why," Nancy said. "We were trying

to find out who set the retreat's jeep on a collision course with a gasoline tanker."

Both Pete and Maddie looked confused. "I don't know what you're talking about," Pete shot back. "But I don't like being accused of things."

"Neither do I," Maddie said angrily. "And I don't like people eavesdropping on my conversations."

"Nancy is just trying to help," Rachel said. "And I'm sure she didn't mean to offend you. We just want some answers."

"Has anyone else been here this morning?" Nancy asked.

"Not that I've seen," Pete said with a shrug. "I've been here for the last hour or so, feeding and brushing horses. Maddie just came over to see if we'd ever figured out how the fire started. Now, what happened with the jeep?"

George and Rachel took turns telling about the runaway jeep and how Nancy had stopped it just in time.

Nancy watched Maddie and Pete's reactions to the story closely. Maddie, she thought, looked both shocked and concerned. Pete had put on a poker face that gave Nancy no clue as to what he was thinking.

"You'd better go check out that jeep," Maddie said to Pete when the story was finished. "I need to check on my birds." Then she turned back to Nancy and Rachel. Her voice was even and low. "I did see a rig parked by the road when I drove up here," she said. "Probably some tourist saw a deer in the meadow."

Nancy thanked her, and the girls left the barn. They hurried toward the dirt road to see if any vehicle was still there.

"Rachel!" Maddie yelled from the barn. "You be careful! This is getting dangerous."

The girls jogged down the driveway and turned onto the dirt road that led to town. Nancy guessed they walked for a quarter mile, but there was no sign of any vehicle. After a fruitless search for tracks they finally gave up and headed back toward the retreat lodge.

"Do you suppose Maddie said that just to get us out of there?" George said. "So that Pete could get rid of any evidence in the jeep?"

"It's a possibility," Nancy said.

"Maddie wouldn't do that," Rachel protested, her face growing red with anger.

"I hope not," Nancy said. "Anyway, I think we need more evidence before we accuse any—"

Nancy's words were suddenly cut off by the sound of a huge explosion!

7

A Startling Truth

"Was that the gas tanker?" George gasped.

"I don't think so," Nancy said, frowning. "It's farther away." Just then she spotted a plume of dust and smoke climbing skyward behind the lodge— from the direction of Miner's Creek.

Rachel gasped, her face pale with fright. "The stream!" she cried, beginning to run in the direction of the blast. Nancy was right behind her, with George and Bess just a few steps back.

The girls reached the lodge and fell into single file as they scrambled down the narrow trail to the stream. The low bushes scratched at their legs and caught their clothing. Rachel seemed not to notice, darting down the trail at top speed, and Nancy wasn't about to fall behind. She knew Rachel might be rushing into a dangerous situation.

When they reached the creek, Nancy quickly saw

what the explosives had been used for. Someone had blown up the dam! A three-foot-wide section was gone, leaving a gaping hole in the middle. Rocks and pieces of concrete were scattered everywhere. Muddy water had rushed into the stream, turning it a milky brown.

Nancy's trained eyes quickly scanned the banks of the stream. Whoever had set the explosives had disappeared.

"The spawning bed is ruined!" Rachel said. She sounded close to tears. "A whole year's work destroyed. And so close to spawning season, too." She stood on the edge of the water, clenching and unclenching her fists. Her eyes grew moist and finally overflowed. Tears trickled down her cheeks.

Nancy was about to wade across the creek to inspect the dam more closely when Charlie rushed down the trail behind her.

"What happened here?" Charlie demanded. "Who did this?"

"We don't know, Granddad," Rachel said with a sniff. "We came as soon as we heard the noise." Charlie put an arm around his granddaughter's shoulder.

"Someone blew up the dam?" Pete sounded shocked as he, too, arrived at the scene.

Nancy wondered if Pete's surprise was all an act. He could easily have set the charge himself after the girls had left to look for the vehicle.

"Yes," Nancy told him. "Do you have any idea who might have done this?"

She watched Pete's reaction closely. His face clouded over immediately.

"That better not be an accusation," he said, frowning. "I was up taking care of that fool jeep."

"What's wrong with the jeep?" Charlie asked. His body grew tense with anger as Pete and Rachel told him about the runaway jeep and the near-explosion. Rachel added that they had looked for a vehicle seen near the meadow. Then Pete told Charlie about untangling the rope from the jeep's steering wheel and returning the jeep to its place by the barn.

"This is getting way out of hand," Charlie said. "I'm calling the sheriff right now."

"Good idea," Nancy said, and Charlie started back up the hill.

Nancy turned to the others. "In the meantime, let's look around here for clues."

George, Bess, and Pete began to search the creek bank while Nancy and Rachel used the fallen tree to cross to the opposite side. Nancy had just jumped to the ground when she heard another small explosion.

She turned to see George fall backward as a small puff of smoke rose from the rocks in front of her. George landed on a mossy rock and slipped into the creek.

"George!" Nancy yelled as she splashed into the water after her friend.

Pete was in the water almost as quickly, and together they helped George to her feet.

"I'm okay," George said, trying to laugh. "I needed a swim, anyway, after all the running around we've been doing."

"You're a good sport, George, but whoever's doing all these things certainly isn't," Nancy said, wading out of the cold water. Rachel had scrambled across the log. She offered a hand to Nancy, and Bess helped George, as the two girls climbed up from the creek, their wet tennis shoes slipping on the round rocks of the bank.

Nancy immediately searched the ground where George had been standing. On one rock she found a black, smoky mark. Near the mark was a small piece of metal. Nancy picked it up as Pete knelt down beside her.

"Copper," he said. "It looks like what's left of a blasting cap. Whoever set that explosion off must have dropped it."

"On purpose?" Bess asked.

"Maybe," Nancy said slowly. "But it probably fell when they were hurrying away."

"What made it go off next to me?" George said.

"Blasting caps go off easily if they're bumped," Pete explained. "You might have kicked a rock onto it or something."

"What exactly are blasting caps used for?" Nancy asked.

"They set off other explosives, like dynamite," Pete told her. "Usually, it's attached to a fuse and dropped inside a stick of dynamite. Then the

56

person lights the fuse. When it burns down, the blasting cap blows up and sets off the dynamite."

"How much time would a person have to get away after the fuse was lit?" Nancy asked.

"Oh, ten or fifteen minutes. More if they made the fuse longer," Pete said.

"We'd better be careful," Nancy said. "There could be more blasting caps around here." She slipped the piece of copper into her pocket. But after twenty minutes of searching on both sides of the creek, no more clues were discovered.

"I don't think we're going to find anything more here," Nancy said with a sigh.

"How about lunch, then?" Bess suggested.

"Uh-oh," Rachel said. "I'm supposed to be helping Elsa fix it. I hope she's not mad."

The group headed up the trail in silence. When they reached the top, Pete headed to the barn, saying he still had chores to finish. George went to the cabin to change into dry clothes. Nancy quickly changed her shoes, then joined Bess and Rachel as they walked across the clearing in front of the lodge. They passed little Aaron Kauffman, who was "mining" for gold in a pile of dirt.

On the porch of the lodge the girls were greeted by Tyler, who was reading with his feet propped up on the railing. He looked fresh and clean, but Nancy noticed that the bottoms of both trouser legs were water-marked. Could he have been wading in Miner's Creek? And if so, could he have been near the spawning grounds?

"Aaron said there was 'a big boom' here a while ago," Tyler said pleasantly as they approached. He laid the book in his lap. "Do any of you know what it was?"

"It was my dam." Rachel spoke in a level but quiet voice. "Someone blew it up."

Tyler pulled his feet off the railing and sat up straight. He pushed his reading glasses up on his head and looked suddenly concerned.

"Another disaster?" Tyler said.

"Looks that way," Rachel said with a sigh. "Someone's really out to get us."

"Is the spawning bed damaged?" Tyler asked. "That *is* an important consideration to the state buying this land, you know. With so many of the salmon runs threatened, protecting them is a top priority with the government."

Rachel fell quickly silent. Too late, she had realized that she was giving Senator Callihan's aide information that could stop the land sale.

"There's been some damage to the spawning bed," Nancy said lightly, trying to ease Tyler's concern. "But Rachel can repair it before the salmon come upstream. Right, Rachel?"

"Right," Rachel said, but she sounded uncertain. "I'd better go and apologize to Elsa for being late for kitchen duty." She pushed open the screen door and headed inside the lodge.

"We're asking everyone if they've seen any strange activity by the creek this morning," Nancy said. She looked pointedly at Tyler's pant legs. "Looks like you were in the creek."

"Just behind my own cabin," Tyler said with a shrug. He looked slyly at Nancy. She was sure he'd guessed what she was getting at with her questioning. "I was looking for some black sand," Tyler went on. "And before that I was in town buying this book. I suppose that's why I didn't hear the blast myself." He held up a book with a bright gold cover, titled *Prospecting History and Methods.*

"I thought you weren't interested in gold," Nancy said.

"I'm not, but Senator Callihan is. I mentioned the story about that lost gold mine, and he said he wanted more information for his report. If there *is* gold on the property, that could complicate our making it a park. Some people think gold should be mined, and that wouldn't be allowed on park land." Tyler closed his book and handed it to Nancy. "I've read enough. Maybe you'd like to take a look at it yourself. You seem to be interested in things like that."

"As a matter of fact, I would like to read it," Nancy said. "It should make our ride to Prospector's Canyon tomorrow more interesting."

She took the book and followed Bess inside for a lunch of chicken salad sandwiches and fresh peaches with milk.

"I thought Bess would appreciate some 'tame' food today," Elsa teased.

Bess's face turned red as she remembered the venison episode the night before.

Everyone was still eating when the sheriff's deputy arrived. Nancy gave him the remains of the blasting cap and told him what she knew about the near-disaster with the jeep. Charlie left his lunch to take the deputy to see the ruined dam. Nancy decided not to go along. She was pretty sure the deputy wouldn't find any more clues, and she knew she could get a report from Charlie later.

"I have to help Elsa for a while," Rachel said when they had finished their sandwiches. "I guess you guys are on your own for the rest of the afternoon."

"That's okay," Nancy said. "I'm going to read this book about prospecting."

"There are some hammocks in the trees by Miner's Creek," Rachel said. "It's a perfect spot for reading."

"Sounds great," Bess agreed.

Soon Nancy, Bess, and George were swaying comfortably in large hammocks tied to huge evergreen trees. Miner's Creek babbled gently in the background.

"Nancy, do you have any idea who is trying to stop the sale of the retreat?" Bess asked.

Nancy sighed. "Not really. For the time being, we don't have much to go on."

Bess gazed through the tree branches toward the blue sky. "I think Maddie and Pete are definitely suspects," Bess said. "They both seem to be around when things go wrong. Maddie even showed up at the fire, remember?"

"Yes, but Pete had been in the meadow that morning, too," Nancy said.

"And Pete was taking care of the jeep when the explosives were set," George pointed out.

"Undoing the rope from the jeep's steering wheel and parking it back next to the barn could have been done quickly," Nancy said. "I think Pete could have done that and set the explosive, too. A long fuse would have given him time to circle around behind the lodge before it went off, then come down the trail as though he were coming from the barn."

George nodded. "I guess you're right."

"And then there's Tyler," Nancy said. "I don't know if I believe his story about being in the creek looking for black sand."

"And he could be the one who's been losing the land sale documents in the senator's office," Bess added.

"But if Maddie is telling the truth, there's another suspect," Nancy said. "Someone driving the vehicle she saw by the retreat's driveway."

"That's true. And we did see tire tracks near the fire," George said. "So where does that leave us?"

"Tired," Bess said.

Nancy and George laughed, and then all three fell silent. George and Bess were soon lulled into sleep by the gentle rustle of the breeze in the pine trees. Nancy concentrated on her book. It was filled with fascinating stories of lost mines and the tricks old prospectors used to protect their secrets.

Suddenly she jumped from her hammock, startling her sleepy friends. Bess nearly fell out of her hammock.

"What is it?" George asked anxiously.

"I'm not sure," Nancy answered. "But I have an idea."

Nancy dashed to their cabin, followed by George and Bess. She threw open her suitcase and pulled out the scrap of paper she had found near the fire, examining it carefully.

"Yes!" she shouted, waving the paper in the air triumphantly. "This is going to help us solve the mystery!"

8

Piecing Things Together

"What do you mean?" George asked.

"I know what this slip of paper is," Nancy said. "It's a report from an assay laboratory, where rocks are analyzed for different minerals. I bet this is an analysis for gold on a rock from the retreat. Look." Nancy showed the girls a page that had an example of an assay report.

Then Nancy set the small scrap of paper she'd found near the fire down on top of a larger piece of scratch paper. She began to fill in the missing letters. As she completed the words, it began to look more and more like the example in the book.

"The first line is the date, and the third line is the address of the laboratory," Nancy said. "We still don't know the address, but I think I can figure out the rest."

As she scribbled, "say Labo" became "Assay

Laboratory," "eport" became "Report," and "mple #653" became "Sample #653."

"What's 'and Re'?" George asked.

"Maybe it's 'and regarding,'" Bess said.

"I don't think so," Nancy said. "Watch."

She continued to work her pencil. "and Re" quickly became "Highland Retreat."

"Of course," George said. "So it does have some connection to the retreat."

"And because I found it near the fire, I'm betting that the same person who is looking for gold also set the fire," Nancy said, setting down her pencil.

"Then someone really believes there's gold here?" Bess said.

Nancy nodded. "I think someone believes that the legend of Miner's Creek is more than just a tall tale."

"But why set the fires?" George still looked confused.

"Remember what Tyler said about the retreat becoming a park?" Nancy said.

"No prospecting or mining would be allowed," Bess finished.

"So there would be park rangers around to make sure no one broke the rules," George added. "If someone is after the gold, they need to stop the land sale."

"Did I hear someone say gold?" a teasing voice came from behind the girls. They turned to see their pilot, B.D. Eastham, standing at the screen door of their cabin.

"Sorry to interrupt," B.D. said cheerfully. "I just stopped by to say hi."

Nancy quickly stuffed the scrap of paper into her pocket and stepped outside to greet B.D.

"We've decided to become prospectors," she said, holding up the book she had been reading.

"Rachel's taking us to Prospector's Canyon tomorrow," George put in. "We're all planning to strike it rich."

"You know a lot of history about this area," Nancy said to B.D. "What do you think of the legend of Miner's Creek? Do you believe it?"

B.D. folded his arms. "You bet," he said with a wink. "Just like I believe in the tooth fairy."

"Then you think it's all a hoax?" Bess said.

"Let's just say I don't think you should waste your vacation looking for gold," B.D. said. "There are plenty of other things to do around here."

"What brings you here today?" Nancy asked, casually changing the subject.

"Oh, I brought up some supplies and mail for Charlie," he said.

"I think he's still with the sheriff," Nancy told him.

B.D. raised his brows. "The sheriff? Has something happened?" he asked.

"Just a fire, an explosion, and a runaway jeep," George said.

"Was anyone hurt?" B.D. asked.

"Not so far," Nancy said.

"It seems like a lot of things have gone wrong

since Charlie started talking about selling this place for a park," B.D. said. "Maybe he should just give it up."

"Give up what?" Charlie came up beside B.D., sounding happy to see his good friend. The sheriff's deputy was with him.

"I was just looking for you," B.D. said. "I've got some mail. By the way, I hear you've had more trouble."

"I'm afraid so," Charlie said. "The deputy here wanted to ask Nancy a question or two before he left. He's been looking into things."

"Any clues as to who set the explosives and sabotaged the jeep?" Bess asked the deputy.

The deputy shook his head. "Unfortunately, I haven't found much to go on. Charlie said he kept a key in the jeep's ashtray, so most anyone could have started the vehicle," he said. "Nancy, when you got to the jeep, did you see anything or take anything out of the jeep?"

"No, I didn't take anything," Nancy said. "Did you talk to Pete?"

"Yes," the deputy said. "He showed me the board and rope. There was nothing else to go on, and I didn't find any usable fingerprints." He turned to Charlie. "I don't know what more I can do than file a report. Call me if anything else happens."

The deputy walked to his patrol car, and Charlie and B.D. strolled toward the lodge.

The girls were soon back in their hammocks. Nancy began poring over the pages of her book again.

"It shows a picture here of a gold nugget the size of a walnut," Nancy reported to Bess and George. "It only weighs three ounces, but it could be worth more than a thousand dollars, even more to collectors because it's an unusual shape."

"And that's for one nugget," Bess said. "Think what a whole gold mine could be worth."

"Millions," Nancy said. "And there's a story here from an old newspaper about a ton of gold that was mined from one ore pocket."

Just then Rachel walked down from the lodge. "So what happened while I was away?" she asked, leaning against one of the trees. "Are you guys having a nice rest?"

George quickly told Rachel what Nancy had discovered about the piece of paper she'd found in the meadow.

"I think someone who believes the story of Jeremiah Benner's mine is hunting for gold here and trying to sabotage the land sale," Nancy said. "Someone doesn't want the gold protected in a park." She sat up on the edge of her hammock. "Rachel, are there any papers or letters from Jeremiah and Cyrus's prospecting days that aren't up on the wall?" Nancy asked. "Anything besides what we've already seen?"

"Well, there are some things left in a box in

Granddad's desk," Rachel said, twisting the end of her ponytail thoughtfully. "He just put the best stuff up for guests to see."

"Maybe we could find another clue if we looked at the box," Nancy said.

The girls followed Rachel back to the lodge. She pulled a cardboard box from a drawer of the large rolltop desk, and the four of them settled down on the hearth of the giant fireplace to sort through old deeds, marriage licenses, and letters. One slightly blurry picture showed Jeremiah and Cyrus together.

"Granddad said that was taken when they first became partners," Rachel said. "Too bad it's not a better picture."

Nancy could just make out the twin white rocks each man held. She guessed they were the two pieces of quartz ore that Jeremiah had brought out of the mountain on the day he'd found the mine.

"Do you see anything that will help?" Rachel asked, after nearly an hour of searching.

"I'm afraid not," Nancy said, shaking her head. "It seems like we have lots of information, but not many solid clues."

"I hope you won't give up," Rachel said.

"Don't worry about that," said Bess with a grin. "Nancy never gives up on a mystery."

The girls carefully placed the papers and photographs back in the box while Rachel went to help Elsa fix dinner. Soon they were all seated around the long table, listening to B.D.'s lively stories about wild plane rides and old fur traders. He was a natural storyteller, and he made dramatic gestures with his hands as he talked. A good actor, Nancy thought.

"It's nice you could stay for dinner," Charlie said to B.D. "With all the problems we've been having lately, good friends make especially good company."

The Kauffmans seemed to be enjoying B.D.'s stories as well, especially little Aaron. He was busily making airplane noises over his plate.

The honeymooning Smythes, Nancy noticed, seemed to be more interested in each other than in B.D.'s wild stories.

"Are you coming with us to Prospector's Canyon?" Aaron asked B.D. "We're going to find a lost gold mine."

"What time?" B.D. asked.

"Ten o'clock sharp," Rachel said. "I'm playing guide."

"I'm afraid I have to work," B.D. said. "But my guess is you'll be disappointed about the gold, anyway. The only gold up there is fool's gold."

Nancy thought it was rude of B.D. to ruin Aaron's hopes so needlessly, especially since B.D. himself was such a good storyteller. But she said nothing, and Aaron seemed not to notice as he continued to make airplane sounds.

After dinner B.D. excused himself, ruffled Aaron's hair playfully, and started for the door.

"I'm going to go get a sweater from the cabin," Nancy said.

"I'll come with you," George said. They accompanied B.D. to the door.

"That was quite a plane ride you gave us the other day," Nancy said casually. "Was it as rough when you flew Tyler in later that evening?"

B.D. hesitated, as though trying to remember.

"Tyler came the night before," B.D. said finally. "His flight was smooth as silk."

"But he didn't arrive here at the retreat until the next night," Nancy said, frowning.

"He stayed in town a day, I believe," B.D. said. "I offered to drive him to the retreat, but he said he was staying over and would rent a car."

Nancy's eyes widened as B.D. said good night and walked to his pickup truck.

"Tyler lied," Nancy said to George as B.D. started his pickup. "He was in town the morning of the fire."

9

Ride into Danger

George followed Nancy back into the lodge, where the other guests were still talking around the big table.

"You know, I think I'll skip the sweater and just go back to the cabin to get some rest," Nancy told everyone. "After all that's happened today, I'm beat."

Rachel was telling the group about a pair of red-tailed hawks nesting on the other side of the meadow. Bess looked up from a cup of steaming tea. Nancy had a feeling her friend wasn't ready to budge from her comfortable chair.

"I guess we'll *all* need our rest for the ride up Miner's Creek tomorrow," she said, hoping Bess would realize that she wanted to talk.

"Nancy's right," George said quickly. "I think I'll turn in, too. Coming, Bess?"

Bess took one last longing look at her sweet-smelling tea and agreed that it was time for bed.

The three filed out of the lodge and headed back to their cabin.

"Okay, what's up?" Bess asked when the door was finally closed.

"Tyler lied," Nancy said. "B.D. said Tyler flew into town the day *before* we did. That means Tyler was here when the fire started."

"And he was the one with the book on gold prospecting," George said, flopping down on her bunk. "Do you think he's trying to find the gold for himself?"

"He's certainly moving up on our list of suspects," Nancy said.

"But is there really any gold?" Bess asked, throwing up her hands. "Tyler isn't the only one who says the story about Jeremiah's mine is a hoax. Charlie and B.D. think the same thing."

"But Tyler could be lying to cover up his real interest," Nancy said.

"Well, if there *is* a gold mine, why wouldn't it have been found after all these years?" George asked.

"It could be underground," Nancy said slowly. "According to that book Tyler loaned me, the quartz and gold were left here by ancient volcanoes." She picked up the book and flipped through the pages. "'Sometimes the gold is visible in long veins that can be followed along a hillside,'" Nancy read. "'But gold can also be found in pockets, many

72

of them underground. Some pockets are the size of a fist. Others are the size of a large room.'" She stopped at a page in the book that showed a diagram of a mountain and the placement of gold pockets. She handed the open book to George.

"But how would Jeremiah have found the gold in the first place?" Bess asked.

"Mostly luck," Nancy said. "But also some detective work. Pocket miners searched for pieces of gold ore on the ground and made a mark on a map for every spot where they found it. That way, by connecting the dots, they could start to form a trail of gold ore."

"So the pocket of gold was at the end of the trail," George said, looking at the diagram.

"Yes, if they were lucky enough to find it," Nancy said. "Like the pot of gold at the end of the rainbow, I guess."

"Maybe we could use the same method to find the gold ourselves," George suggested.

Nancy shook her head. "That would take months, or even years. Besides, if Jeremiah picked up the pieces of ore, there wouldn't be a trail for us to follow," she said.

"Oh, well," George said with a shrug. "The ride up Miner's Creek tomorrow should be interesting, anyway. Who knows, we might get lucky, too."

"Right," Nancy said. "And there's one other thing I want to do in the morning. Remember that second offer that Charlie got for his land?"

"You mean from the preservation group?"

73

George asked. She closed the book and set it back on the nightstand.

"Yes. I want to get some background on them," Nancy said. "And while I do that, you two can check on the other guests and Elsa Parker. We might as well see who has alibis for all of these incidents."

"I guess you were right when you said we'd need to be rested for tomorrow," Bess said, as she pulled on pajamas. "With all the investigating we've got planned, we'd better get to sleep."

"Agreed," George said. "That bunk is looking pretty good to me."

Bess and George fell asleep quickly. Nancy tried, without success, to guess who was out to destroy the retreat. But there were too many possible culprits, and she finally dozed off.

When morning came, Nancy, Bess, and George headed over to the lodge for breakfast. They had agreed that Bess would wait there for the Smythes, and George would try to link up with the Kauffmans when they came in for breakfast. George would talk to Elsa, too.

"Could you use some help in here? I'd love to see firsthand where that wonderful smell is coming from," George said cheerfully as she stuck her head into the kitchen.

Rachel accepted her offer before Elsa had a chance to object.

Nancy and Bess ate jam-filled Danish pastries and

74

finished several glasses of orange juice, which George served with a wink.

"I think George is enjoying her detective work," Bess whispered to Nancy.

"It looks as if you're about to get your turn," Nancy said to Bess as the Smythes walked in the front door of the lodge.

"I'm thinking of taking a walk later," Bess said to Todd and Beth after they had joined the girls at the table. "I have no idea what part of the retreat is best. Do you know a good place to go?" Her friendly show of interest got her an instant invitation from Beth to hear about all of their adventures at Highland Retreat.

Nancy finished her pastry and asked Rachel if she could use the phone in Charlie's office while he was doing errands in town. She pulled the preservation group's letter from her pocket and tried the number printed at the top.

"You've reached the Nature Preservation League," said a man's voice at the other end. Nancy knew immediately that it was a recording, and not a very clear one at that.

"Please leave your name, phone number, and the nature of your business," the voice said.

Nancy hung up quickly and called directory assistance. When she put the receiver down a minute later, her curiosity had been raised. There was no listing for the Nature Preservation League.

Nancy took a few moments to gather her thoughts, then dialed the number on the letterhead a second time. She waited for the beep at the end of the recorded message.

"I'd like to make a rather large donation to your very important cause," Nancy said into the phone. She knew that if the league was legitimate, they would be eager to talk to her. "Please call me to discuss the details."

She gave the phone number of her father's office in River Heights, and then quickly called Carson Drew himself.

"Nancy! How are you? And how are Charlie and Rachel?" her father asked when he heard her voice.

"They're having some problems with the sale, I'm afraid," Nancy told him. "That's why I called. I need your help with something."

"Am I getting in on a mystery?" Carson asked with a chuckle.

"Yes, but you'll have to wait for all the details," Nancy said. She told him quickly about the Nature Preservation League and her phone call to them.

"I need to know right away if they return my call," she said. "Oh, and Dad, do you know a Senator John P. Callihan, or his aide, Tyler Nelson?"

"Sorry, I'm no help there. Washington State is a long way from River Heights," Carson said. "I suppose you want me to check on them, too."

"Thanks, Dad. You're the best." Nancy said goodbye and hung up the phone. Then she replaced the preservation group's letter in the desk. She was deep in thought when George tapped on the door and stepped into Charlie's office.

"Elsa said she was in the kitchen all day yesterday," George told Nancy in a low voice. "And I believe her. She made those rolls from scratch. Plus three blueberry pies for dinner tonight, and homemade croutons for the salad."

"You're right. That probably wouldn't leave Elsa much time to rig a jeep or blow up a dam," Nancy said. "What about the Kauffmans?"

"They went into town after their early breakfast," George reported. "Aaron told me they got back just in time to hear 'the big boom.'" George used her hands to show how Aaron had described the sound of the dam blowing up.

"That seems to leave them in the clear," Nancy said. "I wonder what Bess found out."

As if on cue, Bess walked through the front door of the lodge. She pulled up a chair beside Nancy and George and began to rub her legs.

"Todd and Beth are in awfully good shape," she said. "I would have been better off helping in the kitchen than trying to keep up with them."

Bess reported that she had invited herself on the Smythes' morning jog through the meadow, but she had made only one short loop before giving up.

"I did see the hawk's nest that Rachel told us about at dinner last night," she explained. "Apparently Rachel had told Todd and Beth about it yesterday morning. They watched the nest all day. They even showed me the small blind they built so the mother hawk couldn't see them."

"It sounds as if we've narrowed down our list of suspects," Nancy said. "And I've got a call in to the Nature Preservation League."

She told Bess and George about her phone calls to the league and to her father, finishing up just as the retreat's big triangle gong sounded.

"That's the signal for our ride up Miner's Creek," George said.

The three girls walked to the barn, where they found a group of horses saddled and waiting. Rachel had just finished tying saddlebags full of lunches on her big brown mare. She directed Nancy toward a palomino named Heather. George took the reins of a black-and-white pinto, and Bess climbed aboard a calm, all-black mount.

Todd and Beth Smythe were already sitting on matching bays. Pete helped Shirley and Frank Kauffman onto their horses, then slid Aaron onto a gentle pony that he guaranteed was "a hundred percent safe."

"Tyler isn't coming?" Nancy asked.

"No, he's busy researching," Rachel explained. "And Charlie doesn't like to ride that much anymore."

"Move 'em out," Pete called when everyone was ready. He stood by the barn and watched as the horses headed up the retreat driveway toward Miner's Creek.

Rachel led the way to a shallow place in the stream, where the horses stopped to take a drink, then waded across. Within minutes the group was climbing into the hills toward Prospector's Canyon, where Jeremiah had found the gold-laced quartz.

Nancy's horse quickly passed the others, except for Rachel's mare.

"Heather likes to lead," Rachel said.

They rode side-by-side until the trail narrowed. Then Nancy went in front. Nancy was enjoying the spectacular view as the trail wound around the side of a steep cliff when she suddenly heard a strange buzzing sound. At the same moment she felt her horse tense. The palomino snorted and reared. Nancy found the saddle horn just as the mare's front legs came back to the ground. Heather jumped sideways, almost losing Nancy, and her back legs slid off the side of the trail. Fighting down panic, Nancy looked down and saw Heather's back hooves scrambling in the loose dirt and rocks of the steep bank. Below them the mountainside dropped away to rocky cliffs. Nancy knew she had to stay in the saddle and hope that Heather could fight her way back onto the trail. If the mare failed, they would both tumble over the cliffs!

10

A Mystery in the Bag

Nancy leaned forward, close to her horse's neck. The shift in her weight was just the help that Heather needed. The mare scrambled back onto the trail, but Nancy quickly realized the danger was not yet over.

On the trail behind her the other horses were close to panic. The buzzing sound seemed to grow louder. Then, with a scream, Bess pointed to the trail ahead.

A burlap bag was lying on its side in the middle of the trail. It was moving and writhing like a living thing, inching its way down the trail toward them. The top of the bag had been tied shut, but a small opening remained. A large snake was halfway out of the bag, wriggling to free itself.

"It's full of snakes!" Bess screamed.

"Rattlesnakes," Rachel said grimly.

Nancy's horse was prancing and jumping, once again coming dangerously close to the cliff.

Calmly Rachel ordered everyone to turn their horses around. The group started back down the trail.

Finally Nancy steered a frightened and shaky Heather to a safe clearing at the base of the cliffs.

"Rachel, I'd like to know what's going on here," Frank Kauffman demanded angrily when they had all settled their horses. "That was a very dangerous stunt someone pulled."

Shirley had dismounted and was helping Aaron from his horse. The little boy was frightened, and he looked as if he might burst into tears.

"You can't blame Rachel for this," Nancy told Frank. "Why would she sabotage her own trail ride?"

"You know that's right, Frank," Shirley said gently. "She couldn't have known those snakes were there."

"I guess not," Frank said, frowning. "But I'd like to get my hands on whoever did this."

"So would I," Rachel agreed in a weak voice. Her face was pale, and Nancy could see her hands shaking as she toyed with the bridle reins.

Nancy guided her horse next to Rachel's. "I think someone's trying to keep us out of Prospector's Canyon," Nancy whispered.

Rachel looked startled. She had been too concerned about her guests to consider the reasons for the prank. "But why?" she asked.

"I don't know," Nancy said grimly. "But there's only one way to find out. Is there another route into Prospector's Canyon?"

"Yes, but it's longer. The trail isn't kept up very well, but the horses have been on it before." As she spoke, a look of determination came over Rachel's face. "I'm sure we can make it, Nancy," she added. "Let's get to the bottom of this."

Nancy and George nodded, but Bess seemed reluctant to face any more danger. She listened hopefully as the Kauffmans and the Smythes announced that they were heading back to the barn.

"Maybe you should go back to the retreat, too, Bess. If you don't mind, I mean," Nancy said. "Maybe you can find out who might have gotten up here this morning and planted those snakes."

"I guess I could do some more detecting," Bess said, sounding relieved. She turned her horse back toward the retreat.

"And tell Pete and Granddad about the snakes," Rachel called after Bess.

The trail that Rachel, George, and Nancy followed wound through the forest. The girls had to duck under low-hanging branches of trees that grew close to the trail. The horses trotted along an old logging road for part of the distance. Rachel pointed out a side road that led past Maddie's hospital, then back to the road leading to town.

The trail wound back to Miner's Creek, and the rushing water made it difficult for the girls to hear

82

one another talk. Nancy was surprised that the same stream that flowed gently through the meadow could have so much power in the mountains.

Finally the trail turned away from the stream and passed through a quiet clearing.

"This is a good place for lunch," Rachel announced, jumping off her horse. "We have one more steep climb before we get to the canyon."

Nancy and George dismounted, and the three girls quickly ate a lunch of roast beef sandwiches, corn chips, and lemonade.

"Eat all you want," Rachel told them. "Elsa and I fixed enough for the whole camp, and I didn't think of sending any of it back with the others. I guess I made more work for Elsa. She'll probably fix a second lunch for everyone now."

"I'm sure she'll understand, if we can solve this mystery and end all the problems at the retreat," Nancy said. She hoped they'd find something in the canyon to make their trip worthwhile.

The girls hurried through lunch and mounted their horses again. After a short, rocky climb the trail wound back to the stream and the mouth of a narrow canyon.

Below them the stream cascaded down a rocky slope in a series of small waterfalls. At the top of the falls a large, rocky crag stretched skyward.

"That rock looks like a sand castle," George said, shielding her eyes against the sun as she looked up. "It even has little points at the top."

"That's exactly what I think it looks like," Rachel agreed. "I call it Castle Rock. It guards the entrance to Prospector's Canyon."

The canyon had high, steep sides covered with trees and mountain grasses. At the bottom the stream was once again calm and peaceful. Twisted trees stood like sentries next to small, quiet pools.

Near the creek was a broken chute. Rachel explained that the chute had once been used by prospectors to wash sand.

"It's called a sluice box," Rachel told Nancy and Bess. "It works just like a pan, but it can wash more sand at a time. The miners put sand in one end and let the water wash it down. Black sand and gold would catch behind the ridges on the floor of the chute. Then the miners could collect it easily."

"Is this how Jeremiah mined?" George asked.

"No. Whoever built this chute was a 'placer miner,'" Rachel answered. "Placer miners looked for bits of gold that had broken loose from the main deposit and washed down here. Jeremiah was a 'hard rock' miner. He would have searched the hillsides for the source of the gold—the mother lode."

Nancy got off her horse and examined the chute carefully. "It doesn't look as if it's been used for years," she said. "And I don't see anything here that anyone would want to keep hidden."

"Me, neither," George agreed. "Why do you suppose someone was so determined to keep us from coming here?"

"There must be something," Nancy said. "Let's ride a little farther."

After climbing back on her horse, Nancy let Heather lead the way along the creek. Soon the brush and trees gave way to a combination of rocks and gravel, with only a small tree growing here and there. The open hillside led up to a wall of rocky cliffs. Nancy immediately spotted several fresh holes in the graveled soil.

"Someone's been digging!" Rachel exclaimed.

"Look how the holes seem to make a pattern on the hillside," George added. "They make rows, both up and down and across."

"As if someone's looking for something and following a pattern to cover all the ground," Nancy said.

She tied Heather's reins to a tree and walked up the hillside. The holes were about two feet deep. She was soon joined by Rachel and George.

"Do you know what we're looking for?" Rachel asked.

"No, but there's got to be something more here," Nancy replied. "I'm sure of it."

She was searching through a thick growth of bushes near one of the holes when she caught a glint of metal. Carefully Nancy uncovered a large pick and shovel and a small leather pouch.

"I've found something!" she called to the other girls. Rachel and George gathered around as Nancy opened the pouch and removed a piece of notebook paper with an outline of the hillside drawn on it.

Lines crisscrossed the picture, with *X*'s drawn where each pair of lines came together.

"I bet there's an *X* for every hole dug on the hillside," Nancy said.

Rachel took the picture and counted the holes in the row closest to them.

"I think you're right," she said.

"Someone must be looking for Jeremiah's gold," Nancy said.

"But who? And how are they getting out here without being noticed?" Rachel asked, handing the paper back to Nancy. "The only trails that lead here are the two that we took today. They both start right by the lodge."

"But what about the logging road we followed?" Nancy reminded her. "Didn't you say it passed by Maddie's bird hospital?"

"That's right," Rachel said. "And then it runs into the road to town. I guess that means anyone could have come up that way."

Nancy and George exchanged glances.

"I hope you two don't think Maddie's in on this whole thing," Rachel said, kicking a rock in frustration. "I'm telling you, she's not like that."

"I think we should talk to her, anyway," Nancy said. "Maybe Maddie's seen something."

"I guess a visit would be a good idea," Rachel said finally. "I can take you over tomorrow morning."

"Good," Nancy said. "Let's leave things just as

we found them. And not a word to anyone about our being here."

Nancy replaced the pouch in the bushes, and the girls headed down the hillside. Neither the gravel of the hillside nor the hard, dry soil of the trail held any footprints. Nancy was sure that whoever had been mining in the canyon would not be able to tell they had been there.

When the girls cantered their horses up to the barn, they quickly dismounted, eager to get some dinner. Walking up to the lodge, they found Bess waiting on the porch. Nancy could tell from the way her friend was fidgeting that she had news.

"You won't believe what I found out!" Bess said excitedly. "I think I've solved the mystery."

11

A Rock-Solid Clue

"You mean, you know who's been doing all the damage at the retreat?" Nancy asked in surprise.

"That's right," Bess said, grinning with satisfaction. "And one of them is in the lodge right now, talking to Charlie in his office."

Nancy, Rachel, and George exchanged glances as they walked into the lodge. Charlie's office opened onto the balcony, overlooking the main room where the girls were standing. Nancy considered leading everyone back to their cabin, where they could talk in private, but Rachel nodded for them to follow her to the kitchen.

"Elsa goes into town to meet her sister on Thursday nights," Rachel explained as the girls entered the large, empty kitchen. "And Pete always takes the guests to town for a movie."

Rachel flipped on the lights, and the girls gathered around a small counter in the center of the room, waiting for Bess to tell her story.

Bess took a deep breath. "Okay," she began. "It started when we got back early. Pete was unsaddling a horse—a sweaty horse that looked as if it had been ridden hard. And later I saw Pete talking to Tyler by Tyler's cabin. They broke apart as soon as they saw me. I don't know what they were saying."

Nancy nodded. "It sounds as if those two could be working together. Pete knows the layout of the retreat. He could easily have set up all the accidents, with Tyler's help."

"Wait, there's more," Bess said, touching Nancy's arm. "I went back to the barn—just to check on my horse, since I didn't have anything else to do. I was going to give her a handful of grain. But behind the grain can, I found this. . . ."

Bess reached in her pocket and pulled out the piece of gold-laced quartz.

"That's Granddad's ore!" Rachel cried. She took the rock from Bess and held it in both hands. "But why do you suppose it was in the barn?"

Nancy thought for a moment. "Can you tell if any pieces have been chipped off the rock?" she asked. "Maybe someone wanted an assay report on the ore."

Rachel frowned and turned the piece of quartz slowly in her hand. "It looks the same to me," she said, handing it to Nancy. "But I'm not sure I could tell."

Nancy looked at the quartz carefully. There were no signs of scraping or grinding on the rock, but, like many quartz stones, it had so many bumps and angles that it would have been hard to tell if a small piece had been chipped away. She returned the ore to Rachel.

"It doesn't seem to make sense to me that Pete would have taken it," Rachel said.

Nancy didn't answer. Her impulse was to agree with Rachel, but no one spent as much time in the barn as Pete.

Bess's eyes had wandered to a plate of brownies on the kitchen counter. "Maybe we'll be able to think better after a snack," she suggested.

Nancy suddenly remembered that they hadn't eaten dinner yet. "I'm pretty hungry," she said. "But I'm afraid I'll be just as baffled after I eat as I am right now."

Rachel sighed and slipped the piece of gold ore into her pocket. Then she led the girls to a large refrigerator, where they found leftover roast turkey and potatoes.

"Wait until the barbecue tomorrow," Rachel said. "Elsa's fixing a special roast."

Rachel had told the girls that Charlie had planned the special event in honor of their visit. He had invited all the guests at the retreat. Maddie and B.D. were coming, too.

"I can't wait," Bess said. "Nothing would keep me away from a barbecue."

Rachel set containers of food on a long white

counter by the refrigerator. George and Nancy filled stoneware plates with turkey, corn, mashed potatoes, and gravy. Then they placed the plates in the microwave to heat, one by one, as Rachel pulled up stools around the center counter. Bess watched the others eat as she munched on a piece of celery.

Nancy was just taking her last bite of corn when a huge crash sounded from the main room of the lodge. Nancy rushed through the swinging Dutch doors, followed by George, Rachel, and Bess.

The floor was littered with scattered artifacts from Charlie's historical display. A large framed picture of an old-time prospector lay facedown on the floor, and a pair of saddlebags that had hung on the wall was thrown carelessly in a corner. Looking through a window facing the front of the lodge, Nancy saw the dark figure of a man running down the porch steps.

"Stop!" Nancy ordered as she darted across the big room, jumping lightly over a prospector's pan. She pulled open the front door, hoping to catch another glimpse of the fleeing figure, but the porch was deserted.

Nancy hurried down the steps, colliding with a tall, sturdy man. It was B.D. Eastham.

Nancy was hit so hard that she fell backward. She would have tumbled onto the steps if B.D. hadn't reached out and grabbed her arm.

"Whoa, there, Nancy," B.D. said as he helped Nancy catch her balance. "What's the hurry?"

"I—I was looking for someone," Nancy stammered, stepping backward. "Someone who just ran out of the lodge." Nancy looked at B.D. suspiciously. He seemed to have come out of nowhere. "Have you seen anyone?" she asked.

"No. I just walked around here from my car beside the lodge," he said, pointing toward the corner of the building. "And I didn't see anyone till I ran into you—or you ran into me." He grinned and pushed his hands into his pockets.

"Are you here to see Charlie?" Nancy asked.

"Yup." B.D. looked at the lighted dial on his watch. "It's nine o'clock. I'm right on time."

Nancy remembered that Charlie and B.D. played cribbage every Thursday. She watched B.D.'s face closely in the dim glow of the porch light. He wore his usual cheerful smile. Nancy felt a little embarrassed for having run into him.

"Coming back in?" B.D. asked, gesturing for Nancy to go ahead of him.

Nancy turned around and stepped back through the front door of the lodge. Inside, George, Bess, Rachel, and Charlie were stacking the papers and framed pictures from the floor.

"What happened here?" B.D. asked, surveying the mess. "It looks as if a hurricane breezed through."

"Not a hurricane," Rachel said. "Did you see anyone, Nancy?"

"Just B.D.," Nancy said. She looked around the room. Someone was missing. "Where's Tyler?" she asked.

"He left for town half an hour ago," Charlie said. "He wanted to put a letter in the mail to the senator so it would go out first thing in the morning."

"I could have taken it in for him," B.D. said.

Charlie shrugged. "I told him that," he said. "But Tyler wanted to take a drive, anyway."

At the same time the four girls looked up from sorting papers and exchanged glances. Tyler didn't have an alibi for the ransacking.

"You all look like you just saw a ghost," B.D. said. "Am I missing something here?"

Rachel nodded. "A real mystery," she told him. "And it's looking more and more interesting all the time."

Nancy was afraid Rachel was going to say too much. "Don't you think we should let Charlie and B.D. get to their card game?" she said quickly. "We can clean up here. I'd like to look through these things again, anyway."

Nancy waited until Charlie and B.D. had climbed the stairs to Charlie's office and closed the door behind them.

"I think our culprit is getting desperate," she told the others. "Someone has been here, looking for another clue."

Nancy was silent for a moment, then she looked at Rachel. "Do you think Jeremiah could have hidden a map somewhere?"

"I've never heard of one, but it's possible," Rachel said. "Jeremiah was pretty secretive." She picked up a framed photo and began to examine the back. "Maybe there's some kind of map among these things."

The four girls were soon busy checking every possible place for a clue. As they searched, Nancy, George, and Rachel filled Bess in on their own discoveries.

"It sure has been a busy day," Bess said.

"We've added some pieces to the puzzle, but nothing absolutely proves that Pete and Tyler are our culprits," Nancy said. "After all, anyone could have hidden the ore in the barn. Maybe someone didn't want to be caught with the evidence and figured the barn would be safe."

"But look at the other evidence," George said, examining a large workhorse collar. "Pete was in the meadow the day of the fire. He was near the jeep when it was rigged to run into the tanker. And he took a horse out this morning, just before we found the rattlesnakes."

"But we know Tyler lied about when he flew into Eagle Point," Bess said. "And he left here tonight just half an hour before we found all these things taken down. He had the perfect opportunity to 'lose' the documents Charlie sent to the senator, too."

"And don't forget the book about prospecting," Rachel added.

"But Maddie could have done all those things, too," Nancy said, glancing up from some papers.

Rachel looked hurt. "It's hard to think of Maddie

or Pete trying to harm us," she said. "I still can't believe either of them is involved."

The girls worked in silence. Nancy didn't want to say anything more to upset Rachel, who looked sad enough as she searched through the items from the historical display. As the mood in the room grew more and more gloomy, Nancy saw the need to liven things up. She leaned back on her heels and declared cheerfully, "I think we need a new approach."

The other girls looked at Nancy with interest.

"What if there's a clue here, and it was hidden by Jeremiah himself?" Nancy said. "Where do you think it would be?"

The silence returned as each of the girls looked around again at the objects on the floor. Nancy reached for a fringed leather jacket and checked it carefully for secret pockets or papers hidden in the lining.

"Nothing," she said.

George leafed through the book she was holding a second time, and Rachel checked a set of old saddlebags for secret compartments. Both girls came up empty-handed.

Then Nancy reached for Jeremiah's pick, which had hung above Charlie's quartz stone. She examined it from top to bottom, finally focusing on the end of the handle.

"It looks as if this has been cut," she said. "Like someone hollowed out the handle and then fit another piece of wood in the hole."

"You're right, it does," Rachel agreed, looking over Nancy's shoulder. "How can we get it out?"

"I have an idea," Nancy said. She got to her feet and hurried toward the kitchen, carrying the pick. There, she took two forks from a drawer and handed the pick to Rachel. "Hold this at an angle," she instructed her. Then Nancy eased the prongs of the forks into the edge of the wooden plug in the center of the handle, one on each side. She wiggled them until the piece of wood began to work loose.

Bess's eyes widened as Nancy carefully removed the wooden plug. The handle of the pickax was hollow.

"There's something inside," Rachel breathed, leaning closer.

Nancy reached into the handle and pulled out a brittle, yellowed paper. It had been folded many times. She unfolded the paper and laid it on the kitchen counter. She gently flattened it out, holding the corners with her fingers.

Everyone stared at Nancy's find in amazement. It was a map of Prospector's Canyon!

12

X Marks the Spot

Rachel pointed to the roughly drawn map. "Look. This is the waterfall, and this peak with the three points . . ."

"Has got to be Castle Rock," Nancy finished.

"So, what else does the map tell us?" Bess asked.

The girls bent over the paper. It was about six inches square, with several small tears along the edges. Nancy held it carefully as Rachel traced the line labeled Miner's Creek. Then Rachel helped pick out landmarks that George and Nancy recognized from their ride that morning.

"This looks like the cliffs and the open slope we saw today, where the holes were recently dug," Rachel said, pointing to some carefully drawn lines. "It looks as if Jeremiah took extra care drawing this part of the map."

Each rock of the cliffs was clearly outlined. Near

the center of the open hillside, a crevice was shown in the rocks that looked like a shallow cave. An *X* was drawn in the center of the opening.

"I don't remember any caves in that cliff," Nancy said, frowning.

"Neither do I," Rachel said. "But this map was made almost a hundred years ago, and there are a lot of loose rocks on those cliffs. There could be caves that have been covered up by rock slides."

"Do you think that's what happened to Jeremiah's gold mine?" George asked. "Could it have been covered up by a rock slide so that no one could find it?"

"Maybe," Nancy said slowly, tapping the map. "Or Jeremiah might even have covered the cave himself to hide the mine. Maybe he was planning to come back later and finish mining."

"But how can we know for sure that this *X* means a gold mine?" Bess asked.

"We can't," Nancy said. "Not without going back to Prospector's Canyon and doing some digging of our own. In the meantime, maybe we can use this map to catch a crook." She looked around at the others. "Let's not tell anyone what we've found until I can think of a way to use it," she cautioned. "Not even Charlie." Nancy held Rachel's gaze for an extra moment. She wanted to be sure she could count on her new friend to keep the secret.

"Okay, but only for a while," Rachel agreed finally. "After all, it is Charlie's land."

"I understand," Nancy said. "Now, let's finish cleaning up."

Nancy refolded the map, taking care not to rip it more. She placed it in the pocket of her shirt and followed the others back into the main room of the lodge.

The girls quickly rehung pictures and placed objects back on their shelves. Upstairs, the light under the door of Charlie's office told Nancy that he and B.D. were still playing their card game.

"I'm ready for bed," Bess announced as she placed the last picture back on its hook.

"So am I, but I'm not sure I can walk to the cabin," George said, hobbling toward the door. Her legs were already getting stiff from the all-day horseback ride.

"Don't worry," Rachel teased. "It'll be worse tomorrow."

By morning George could hardly lift her legs out of bed. Nancy, too, was stiff from horseback riding, but she had already stretched her legs by the time George got up.

"They loosen up pretty quickly," Nancy assured her friend.

George put one foot on the back of a chair and gently stretched the muscles in her legs. It took her just a few minutes to work out the stiffness. She pulled on shorts and a sweatshirt, and she, Bess, and Nancy headed to the lodge for breakfast.

They found an impatient Rachel hovering around the dining room table, on which scrambled eggs, sausage, and a basket of blueberry muffins were waiting for them.

"I was about to come and wake you up," she called when the girls walked in. When they had crossed the room to the table, Rachel whispered to Nancy, "Do you have a plan for today?"

"I want you to take me to visit Maddie," Nancy told her. "We need to ask her if she's seen anyone drive by her bird hospital. George, you can keep an eye on Pete while we're gone, and Bess, your assignment is Tyler."

The girls agreed, and after a quick breakfast Nancy and Rachel got in the retreat's blue van and headed down the dirt driveway. When they reached the main road, Rachel turned right, in the opposite direction from Eagle Point. Then they drove about a mile to the next turnoff.

"This road leads to both Maddie's house and Prospector's Canyon," Rachel said, steering the van onto a dirt road that wound through the trees. It was several minutes before Nancy spotted a small green house off to the left. The road was heading toward the mountains, but Rachel turned off on a short driveway that led almost to Maddie Emerson's front door.

Maddie was on the porch before the girls even got out of the van. Her "good morning" lacked enthusiasm, Nancy thought, and her smile seemed strained. Her eyes darted back and forth from Nancy to Rachel.

"We just stopped by to chat," Rachel said cheerfully. "How's Rocky?"

"Pretty good, really," Maddie said. Her voice sounded a bit friendlier. "He's still eating, and he's using his wing some now. I think he may even fly again, in a couple more weeks. You can help me release him."

"Rocky is a golden eagle," Rachel explained to Nancy. "His wing was broken."

"Yes, when he was shot by some fool city hunter," Maddie broke in. Her voice was angry again. "And you wonder why I don't want more people around here."

"The birds are lucky to have you as their guardian angel," Nancy said. "I'd love to see Rocky sometime."

Maddie didn't offer to show Nancy the eagle, but she invited both girls inside. Her house was small, not much bigger than the cabins back at the retreat. As she heated water for tea, Nancy let Rachel do most of the talking.

"So, have you figured a way to get an operating room here?" Rachel asked.

Maddie shook her head. "No. I can barely afford the bills to take the birds to the vet, let alone have him come here," she answered.

Rachel explained to Nancy that the trip to the veterinarian in town for surgery was hard on the

101

injured birds. The trips back and forth over the dirt road, and being around the cats and dogs that were always at the vet's, also increased their distress.

"Maddie wants to build a new, bigger place for the birds, but she doesn't have the money right now," Rachel finished.

"There may be a way, though," Maddie said. "I'm working on something."

Nancy waited, but Maddie did not explain her plan. What exactly *was* the woman working on? Nancy wondered.

Maddie grew a bit friendlier as the morning went on. By the time they had finished their tea, Nancy was beginning to understand why Rachel liked the woman so much. She showed a gentler nature to Rachel, and the two of them shared a love for the creatures of the forest.

"Come on, I'll let you see Rocky," Maddie said finally. She led the way to a door at the back of her small house.

"I've also got some baby owls," she said. "A logger cut down the tree their nest was in, poor things, but they're doing better now."

She put her finger to her lips, then slowly opened the door to her hospital.

Nancy quickly saw that the large room was bigger than the part of the house that Maddie lived in. Along the far wall were shelves filled with large and small cages. In one cage two small owls were just losing their baby fuzz.

"That's Rocky," Rachel whispered, pointing. At

the opposite end of the room, a great golden-brown bird sat on a large perch and stared at the human intruders.

Nancy had the uncomfortable feeling that the eagle was looking right through her and that she wasn't welcome in the room. A few moments later Maddie motioned for them to leave, then closed the door silently behind them.

"Rocky looks good," Rachel said to Maddie. "Thanks to you."

"He's magnificent," Nancy said. "I wish I could have gotten a closer look."

"Maddie usually doesn't let people look at her birds at all," Rachel explained, walking toward the door. "There's a real trick to getting them well without making them tame. If they're going to be released into the wild, they can't get too used to people."

"So it's important to keep people away from here?" Nancy said, raising her eyebrows.

"That's right," Maddie said firmly. "People and noise are the worst things for these birds right now."

"So you would probably notice if anyone drove by on the road past your house," Nancy said.

Maddie shrugged. "Maybe. Why?"

Nancy could see that Maddie had grown instantly wary.

"We think someone's coming onto the retreat from a back way," Nancy said, trying to sound friendly. "Maybe from your property."

103

"I've heard a few trucks going by. No more than usual," Maddie said flatly. "Tourists and hunters like to drive these back roads."

Then Maddie's eyes narrowed as she looked sternly at Nancy. "Maybe you're suggesting that I've been trespassing," she said, pushing her chin in the air defiantly. "Rachel, I think you'd better take your friend and go now."

Rachel motioned Nancy to the door. Nancy followed her, wondering why the stocky woman was being so defensive. Nancy decided it would be best to leave. She was saying goodbye to Maddie when her eyes caught the glint of shiny metal.

There, resting on a table near the door, was a small copper blasting cap!

13

A Paper Trail

"What do you use blasting caps for?" Nancy asked, turning to Maddie.

"I found that," the woman shot back angrily. "Now, I really think you should go."

Maddie turned on her heels and strode back toward the bird room.

"We'd better leave," Rachel said.

Nancy quickly stepped out, and Rachel closed the front door behind them. Rachel was very quiet as they got into the van and headed home.

"Do you know what Maddie's working on to get money for her hospital?" Nancy asked.

"Sometimes she gets grants from the government for her work," Rachel said with a shrug. "It's probably something like that."

Nancy wasn't convinced, but she didn't want to hurt her friend. She gazed out the window of the

105

van as they bounced past the endless straight trunks of evergreen trees.

"Rachel, I know you like Maddie," Nancy began gently. "But isn't it possible she could be involved in the problems at the retreat?"

Rachel was silent for a long moment as she steered the van down the road. "I hate to think that Maddie might be involved," Rachel said finally. "But it *is* possible, I guess."

"Maddie's said over and over again that she's against the retreat becoming a park," Nancy reminded her. "Plus, we know she wants more money for a new hospital, and now she says she has an idea for getting it. What if that idea is the Miner's Creek gold?"

"I suppose it does look pretty bad," Rachel said with a sigh. "But what about the blasting at the salmon spawning beds? Maddie would never do a thing like that. She loves animals too much."

Nancy nodded. "You're right. That doesn't seem to fit her nature. But maybe she didn't plan all the disasters herself. She could be working with someone else."

"You mean, like Pete," Rachel said.

"He *is* one of our leading suspects," Nancy said. "Still, I can't shake the feeling that we're missing something—or someone."

Rachel turned the van into the retreat driveway. As they neared the lodge, she slowed down. A pinto horse and rider were walking slowly up the drive in front of them.

"It's George," Nancy said, waving to her friend. Rachel parked the van, and Nancy jumped out.

"I thought you were watching Pete," she said.

"I was," George said. "The only way I could think of to keep an eye on him was by helping him in the barn. After a while he started getting suspicious, so I said I wanted to take a ride. All he did all morning was clean stalls—and help me saddle this horse."

George promised she would take only a short ride and check on Pete again when she returned to the barn.

"I'm going to change into shorts," Nancy told Rachel as George rode away. "It's getting much too warm for these jeans. I'll meet you back at the lodge, okay?"

Rachel nodded, and the two girls went in opposite directions. But as Nancy neared the cabin, she saw that the door had been left ajar. She pushed it open carefully.

The cabin was in turmoil. All of the girls' suitcases had been opened and dumped onto the floor. The beds had been torn up and the drawers opened in the tiny kitchen.

Someone had obviously searched the girls' cabin while they were gone. But what could they have been looking for?

Nancy touched the buttoned pocket of her shirt. The map was still there, thank goodness. She was glad she'd kept it with her. In its fragile condition,

107

she had thought about leaving it hidden in her suitcase.

Nancy sat on one of the bunks and looked around the room, wondering again why anyone would ransack the cabin. What could the intruder have been looking for? No one knew about the map. She had to find out what, if anything, was missing.

The book on prospecting that Tyler had loaned her was right where Nancy had left it on the kitchen counter. She walked over and saw that it had been opened to a page that she had marked on how to find gold.

Nancy closed the book again. Had the pages told the burglar anything new? Probably not.

Nancy reached for the smallest of three canisters that sat on the counter. She had put her only other physical evidence inside of it yesterday. She lifted the lid and found the canister empty. The piece of the assay report was gone!

As Nancy replaced the lid, she wondered if someone had come looking for just that piece of paper. But how had he or she known that Nancy had found it in the meadow? Or maybe the burglar had come across the assay report accidentally while looking for something else. Could whoever it was have guessed that they'd found a map? Someone might have been spying on them last night! That thought sent a shiver up Nancy's spine. She would have to tell George, Bess, and Rachel to be especially careful.

Nancy was picking up clothes from the floor when she heard a moan from the bathroom. Quietly she crossed the room and edged the door to the small room open. There, sprawled on the floor, was a barely conscious Bess. She was lying on her side, her long hair in a disheveled mass on the wood floor.

Nancy knelt down beside her friend as Bess moaned again and started to move. There was a large lump on the back of her head, and a small amount of blood was already dried in her blond hair.

"Nancy, am I glad to see you," Bess said groggily when she opened her eyes. "What hit me?"

"I don't know, but whatever it was, it came down hard," Nancy said. "You've got a nasty lump here."

Nancy gently felt around the back of Bess's head to check her injuries.

"I think you're going to be okay," she said. "Can you stand up?"

"I think so," Bess said.

With Nancy's help Bess managed to get to her feet and walk the few steps to the nearest bunk bed. Nancy helped her lie down.

"Stay still," Nancy told her. "I'm going to get help. But first, tell me what happened."

Bess shook her head slowly. "I'm not sure," she said. "I walked around the grounds for a while this morning, looking for Tyler. I never found him, so I came back here. When I opened the door to the cabin, my suitcase was open. Then I thought I heard a noise in the bathroom. I went in to see what it was, and *wham!*"

"Did you see anyone?" Nancy asked.

"No, nothing," Bess said.

Nancy squeezed Bess's hand and ran toward the lodge. She threw open the front door and yelled for Rachel.

"I'm upstairs," Rachel called as she came out of her room and leaned over the balcony. "What's up?"

"Bess has been hurt," Nancy said. "She was unconscious for several minutes, at least. I think she should see a doctor."

By the time Nancy had finished her explanation, Charlie had come out of his office and started down the stairs, with Rachel right behind him. Elsa pushed open the swinging doors to the kitchen and hurried toward Nancy, drying her hands on her apron.

"Where is she?" Charlie demanded, striding across the room.

"Is she badly hurt?" Elsa asked anxiously.

"She's in the cabin. She was hit on the head—by an intruder," Nancy said.

With Nancy in the lead, the group made a cavalry-style rush to the cabin, all intent on helping Bess. After both Elsa and Charlie had examined her, they agreed Bess should see a doctor.

"I'll drive her to the clinic," Elsa said.

"And I'll go with you." There was a look of determination on Rachel's face as she spoke. "Then we're going to find out who did this, one way or another."

Nancy hoped that Rachel could keep her emotions under control. Rachel would need a clear head to be of any help in solving this mystery.

Rachel was right about one thing, though, Nancy thought. It was time to find whoever was causing all the problems at Highland Retreat. The situation seemed to be becoming more dangerous every day.

Elsa and Rachel were helping Bess up off the bunk when George walked in.

"What's this, a party?" George asked. Then she noticed Bess and quickly became serious. "What happened? What's going on?"

Nancy quickly told the story.

"I just put my horse away," George said. "Pete's not in the barn anymore. He would have had time to do this after I left him. I should have stayed in the barn."

Nancy noticed that Elsa looked shocked that George would accuse Pete, but the cook quickly turned back to Bess, saying nothing.

Charlie was more outspoken. "Pete wouldn't do this," he said firmly. "And I don't like you accusing him."

"It could have been someone else," Nancy said quickly. "Tyler, for instance. Bess told us she never did see him this morning."

"Tyler said he was going to town about an hour ago," Charlie said. "To the post office."

"The post office—again," Rachel said, showing by her tone that she didn't believe his alibi.

"Did you see him leave?" Nancy asked.

"No, but his car is gone," Charlie said.

Nancy turned toward Bess, who was now standing with the help of both Elsa and Rachel. Nancy held the door open as they walked Bess out to the van. Bess slid into the seat behind the driver, with Rachel beside her. Elsa climbed behind the steering wheel.

Nancy was convinced that her friend would be well taken care of. As the van sped down the driveway, Nancy turned to Charlie.

"Could you please take out all the papers that have to do with the sale of Highland Retreat?" she asked him. "If George and I don't meet you in your office in twenty minutes, call the sheriff. We're going to check out Tyler's cabin."

George and Nancy walked quickly toward the government aide's cabin.

"What are we doing?" George whispered as Nancy rapped firmly on Tyler's door.

"Looking for answers," Nancy told her.

Nancy knocked on the door three more times before deciding that the cabin was empty. Carefully she turned the knob. The door was unlocked. After pushing it open just a crack, she called, "Anyone here?"

Still there was no answer. Nancy pushed the door

open the rest of the way, and she and George stepped cautiously inside.

Tyler's cabin was identical to their own. The single room, the bunk beds, small kitchen, and bathroom were all in the same places.

There was a loaf of bread on the counter, and when Nancy opened the tiny refrigerator, she found a quart of milk and some butter.

"I guess that's why we didn't see him at breakfast," Nancy said. "He must have fixed his own here."

Nancy closed the refrigerator and began to look around the rest of the cabin.

"Watch out the window to make sure Tyler isn't coming back," Nancy said to George.

"Okay," George said.

Nancy glanced through another stack of books on the counter. All of them were related to politics. Several weekly news magazines lay on the floor beside the bunk. "This guy is really serious about his work," Nancy muttered.

A pen and some papers lay on a small nightstand. On top of the papers, neatly stacked, were a personal appointment book and a journal.

Nancy opened the journal first, though she expected that Tyler was too clever to write down any wrongdoing. The last entry was dated a week earlier.

She quickly leafed through the papers and stopped when she saw the unusual, three-eagle letterhead of the Nature Preservation League.

"Bingo," she said as she pulled the letter out of the stack. It was a copy of the letter Charlie had shown her.

"What do you suppose Tyler is doing with this?" she wondered out loud.

"Whatever you found, you'd better tell me about it later," George said, ducking away from the window. "Tyler's car is coming up the driveway."

Nancy replaced the letter in the stack. Then she and George hurried to the back door of the cabin.

George reached for the doorknob, but Nancy wouldn't let her open it until she heard Tyler's car in front of the cabin.

"If we leave too soon, he'll see us," Nancy whispered.

Finally, as Tyler walked to his front door, Nancy and George sneaked out the back.

"That was close," George said.

"It sure was, but I think it was worth it," Nancy said. "Let's go meet Charlie, and I'll explain."

The girls walked behind the cabins, then cut across to the lodge. The door to Charlie's office was open, and Charlie was sitting at his desk. In front of him was a small stack of papers.

"Did you give Tyler a copy of the letter from the Nature Preservation League?" Nancy asked.

"No," Charlie replied. "I kept that offer secret, except for telling you. It was my ace in the hole. Why?"

"Well, Tyler has a copy of it," Nancy said.

"Where would he have gotten it?" George asked.

"I don't know—unless he was the one writing it," Nancy said. "I think it's time for another call to Dad."

Nancy waited while the receptionist at Carson Drew's office routed her call through. George and Charlie waited silently.

"Hello, Nancy. No news about your donation," Carson Drew said when he had picked up the phone. "How is everything going?"

"It's slow, but I think we're closing in," Nancy said. She had decided not to worry her dad with the news of Bess's injury.

"I've done a little checking," Carson said. "I couldn't find anyone who'd ever heard of this Nature Preservation League."

"I'm not surprised," Nancy said. "I think it's a front. Someone wants to get his or her hands on this land."

"How valuable is it?" Carson asked.

"Very, especially if there's gold here," Nancy told him. "Did you find out anything about the senator or Tyler Nelson?"

"The senator is a respected legislator," Nancy's father replied. "He's been in office for twelve years and has a scandal-free record. I didn't find out much about Tyler, except that he's from a wealthy Seattle family. Graduated from Stanford University. Now, what's this about gold?"

"It's a long story, Dad. I'll tell you the whole thing when I get home, I promise. But tell me, is Tyler's family wealthy enough to buy the retreat?"

"From what I hear, they are," Carson said. "Apparently Tyler's grandfather founded a shipbuilding firm in Seattle. It's now one of the largest in the country."

"I think you've just helped me solve a mystery," Nancy said.

She thanked her father and promised him that she would be careful. Then she hung up and turned her attention back to George and Charlie, who were waiting impatiently to hear what she had learned.

"Tyler's got money," Nancy said. "Enough to buy this place, if he can stop the government deal. And my father can't trace the Nature Preservation League."

"So you think Tyler's been causing all the problems around here?" Charlie asked.

"It's possible," Nancy said. "But if he did, I suspect he had help. Pete looks like a likely accomplice."

"I'm going to call the sheriff again," Charlie said, reaching for the phone.

"But we don't have any real evidence," Nancy protested. "The only thing I had was that piece of paper from the assay office, and now that's gone. I think we should set a trap."

"That's too dangerous," Charlie said.

"No more dangerous than letting whoever is doing all of this get away, free to come back and cause you more trouble," Nancy argued.

"I suppose you're right." Charlie sat back in his chair and sighed. "But you've got just one chance to bring this culprit out in the open. Then I'm calling in the law."

"It's a deal," Nancy said. She was already forming a plan in her mind.

"Would you make sure Maddie and B.D. are coming to the barbecue tonight?" she asked Charlie. "I think everyone should be here for this."

Charlie agreed, and Nancy laid out her plan. She pulled the folded map from her shirt pocket and showed it to Charlie.

His eyes widened. "What on earth . . . ?" he began.

"We're pretty sure it shows the location of Jeremiah's gold mine," Nancy said, explaining where she had found the map. "And tonight we're going to use it as bait to catch a crook."

Nancy sent George to get a pinch of black sand from the prospecting pan in the display downstairs. While she was gone, Nancy quickly copied the important landmarks on the map, including the rocks of the cliff and the *X*. When George returned, Nancy had her drop the sand in an envelope. Then Nancy folded the map up.

She handed the map to Charlie and put the copy in her pocket. "Tonight at the barbecue, wear a jacket and make sure everyone knows that map is in the pocket," Nancy told him.

Charlie nodded.

"We'll help you find an excuse to come back to the lodge and leave your jacket on the hook," Nancy went on. "But before you hang it up, I want you to take a pinch of sand from this envelope and put it inside the folded map. If that sand is gone when we unfold the map, we'll know someone else has looked at it.

"When you come back to the barbecue without the jacket or the map," Nancy continued, "our crook will know where to look for it. Then, when he goes to Prospector's Canyon to look for the gold, he'll get a big surprise—us!"

14

All Together

Nancy, Charlie, and George had just finished making their plans when they heard the screen door of the lodge swing shut. All three of them hurried to the railing, where they saw Elsa and Rachel below.

"Where's Bess?" George asked as they came downstairs, eager for news. "Didn't she come back with you?"

"She's fine." Elsa's voice sounded tired. "At least, the doctor thinks she's all right, but he wanted to keep her in the hospital overnight—just to be sure."

"Bess didn't get worse after she left here, did she?" Nancy asked anxiously.

"No. Actually, when we were leaving, Bess told us her headache was almost gone," Rachel said. "She was pretty mad about missing the barbecue tonight, too. She seemed to think that Elsa's roast would be a lot better than the hospital food."

119

Nancy smiled. It sounded as if Bess was making a quick recovery.

Elsa leaned toward Nancy. "She also said she bet you'd have something special planned for tonight, Nancy," she said in a low voice. "I hope it's nothing dangerous. I think one girl in the hospital is enough."

Nancy stiffened. "I'm sure that enjoying all that good food will be plenty of adventure for tonight," she said, trying to sound cheerful.

Elsa gave her a suspicious look, then shook her head and pushed through the doors to the kitchen.

"I hope you can help me, Rachel," Elsa said, sticking her head back through the door. "I'm way behind schedule."

Rachel sighed as she started after Elsa.

"We can help, too," Nancy offered. "Taking Bess to the hospital must have put you all behind."

A late lunch was the first order of business in the kitchen. Nancy and George quickly had a large tray of turkey sandwiches ready. Both the Smythes and the Kauffmans had picked up sack lunches at breakfast and left for day-long hikes. Rachel took a sandwich, chips, and a glass of iced tea up to Charlie in his office. George volunteered to help Elsa carry food and a large thermos of iced tea to Pete, who was barbecuing a large roast beef at the pit located near the side of the barn. While they were gone, Nancy filled Rachel in on their plan for the evening as they ate sandwiches at the dining room table.

"Charlie won't be in any danger, will he?" Rachel asked. "This person, whoever it is, has already hurt Bess."

"Charlie will be safe," Nancy assured her. "And we've already agreed to call the sheriff if things get dangerous."

"All right. I have an idea to get Charlie back up here after he shows everyone the map," Rachel said.

Just then Elsa and George came back into the kitchen.

"Pete is turning the roast," George announced. "And that sauce smells delicious."

Under Elsa's direction the apprentice cooks soon had a large potato salad and a platter of fresh fruit ready. Elsa was baking big loaves of French bread that had been rising since morning. The last chore was to toss a large green salad.

When everything was ready, the girls helped carry the food to the barbecue.

The guests had already gathered and were enjoying the perfect summer weather. Maddie Emerson was sitting in a lawn chair near a giant pine tree at the edge of the picnic area. She sat very still, and her head was tilted toward the sky. Nancy guessed that she was listening to the birds that were singing their evening songs in the trees.

B.D. was deep in conversation with Frank Kauffman and Todd and Beth Smythe. His usual smiling face and large, sweeping gestures told Nancy that he was telling another story. Aaron

121

Kauffman stood next to his mother, watching the roast turn slowly over the coals at the barbecue pit. Tyler was looking over the food on the table.

"I wasn't sure Maddie would come after your run-in with her this morning," George whispered to Nancy.

"I wasn't, either," Nancy whispered back. "But I'm glad she did. Now all of our suspects are present."

As soon as the girls had set the food down on one of the large picnic tables, Charlie started to tell his story.

"Since most of you were at dinner the other night and heard the tale of Jeremiah Benner and the Miner's Creek gold," Charlie began, "I thought I would tell you all the sequel to the story." He pulled the folded map from his jacket pocket and held it in the air.

"I have here the map to Jeremiah's hidden gold mine. Before everyone gets excited, I want to say that the map shows a cave in the mountains. I've been all over this retreat since I was a boy, and I can assure you, there is no cave like this. But this map should make a nice addition to my display of mining artifacts. I only wish Jeremiah had autographed it."

The group murmured with excitement. Shirley Kauffman asked Charlie where he had found the map, and Aaron said he wanted to get a look at it. Charlie answered their questions and managed to keep everyone from getting too close to the map.

"It's a bit fragile to pass around," he said. "But

next week I'll get a suitable frame for it, and then you can all have a good look."

Charlie stuck the map back in his jacket and picked up a big pitcher of lemonade.

"Now, who wants a drink of Elsa's famous lemonade?" he said.

Aaron Kauffman was first in line, followed by several of the other guests.

"How'd I do?" Charlie asked Nancy when he got a chance. "Do you think I was convincing?"

"We'll soon find out," Nancy replied. She smiled at Beth Smythe, who was energetically telling Rachel more about the hawk family they had been watching. B.D. came up to talk to Charlie. The other guests had gathered around the fire, sipping lemonade and enjoying the wonderful smell of the cooking roast. Aaron was once again talking about the gold mine, and everyone seemed to be enjoying his childish enthusiasm. But while Charlie's story had sparked interest among the guests, so far no one had shown any suspicious reactions.

By the time Pete announced that the roast was finished, the fresh evening air, the birds' songs, and the wind in the trees had worked their magic. The hungry guests were relaxed and happy. It was a perfect party night, Nancy thought, except for the shadow of trouble hanging over the retreat.

It was time, Nancy thought, for Charlie to slip away and deposit his jacket and its contents in the lodge. Suddenly she heard Rachel shriek.

Nancy looked over to see a splash of barbecue

sauce dribble down the front of Charlie's jacket. Rachel was holding the bowl of sauce that Pete had been using to baste the roast and apologizing profusely to her grandfather. Nancy guessed that Rachel had spilled the sauce on Charlie's jacket on purpose.

"Don't worry about it," Charlie told Rachel. "I'll just run up to the lodge and change."

So that had been Rachel's idea, Nancy thought, making an effort to keep a smile off her face.

"Remember, that has to be dry-cleaned," Rachel called after him loudly. "Just hang it by the door, and I'll take it to the cleaners tomorrow."

"Nice touch," Nancy whispered to Rachel a moment later. "You should be a detective."

"Do you really think so?" Rachel looked pleased. "I hope I didn't overdo it."

"You were perfect," Nancy said. "Our trap is set."

A few minutes later Charlie reappeared, minus his lightweight jacket.

"I was too warm, anyway," he assured Rachel with a wink, then returned to his plate of meat and salad.

Nancy munched on fresh fruit, while George promised her the roast was well worth the calories.

"We should save some for Bess," George said.

But Nancy was too busy watching everyone to eat very much. Finally, with dinner over, Pete excused himself.

"I've got horses to feed and an early day tomorrow," he said.

Nancy watched as he disappeared into the barn. Where he would go from there, she could only guess. In the dark it was impossible to see the lodge from the barbecue area.

Maddie and B.D. were the next to say good night, and the Smythes followed close behind.

"I'd better be going, too," Tyler said. "I've got a plane to catch tomorrow, and I have to finish my report."

Nancy watched Tyler walk away. Then she heard a voice behind her.

"I just wanted to apologize in person for the thing with the quartz," the woman said.

Nancy spun around to see Shirley Kauffman talking to Rachel.

"What do you mean?" Rachel asked.

"About Aaron taking your quartz. I'm really sorry. We had a talk with him about it. He just got all wrapped up in the story about Jeremiah, didn't you, Aaron?" Shirley Kauffman was holding the little boy's hand, and he looked down sheepishly.

"I was prospecting, like Jeremiah Benner," Aaron said.

"Aaron took the quartz?" Rachel said in surprise.

"Why, yes. I told Pete that when I returned it." Now Shirley looked confused. "I was going to bring it back to the lodge, but Pete offered to take it. That was Thursday—after the trail ride."

Rachel stared at Shirley. "It's all right, of course," she finally blurted out. "I'm sure Aaron didn't mean any harm. And thank you . . . for returning it."

Shirley Kauffman nodded and released Aaron's hand. As soon as he was free, Aaron galloped away, waving his arms and shouting, "We're rich, we're rich! I struck it rich!" in what Nancy guessed was an imitation of Jeremiah Benner and his burro hurrying down the mountain.

Shirley Kauffman shook her head in dismay before trotting after her unruly son. Frank followed behind them.

"We may have made a mistake, accusing Pete of taking the quartz," Rachel said, coming up to Nancy. George was right behind her. She'd heard the conversation, too.

"But why didn't Pete say anything?" George asked.

"Maybe he felt there wasn't much to say, once the quartz was gone from the barn," Nancy told her. "Anyway, we'll know soon if he's been involved in any of the incidents."

"What's this about my quartz?" Charlie leaned over Rachel's shoulder.

"Granddad, so much has happened that I haven't had a chance to tell you. Bess found your quartz in the barn. I have it in my room now," Rachel explained. "We thought Pete stole it, but it looks as if we were wrong." She told her grandfather what Shirley Kauffman had just said.

"I guess I can straighten that out tomorrow," Charlie said.

The girls began to help Elsa clean up.

"I suppose," Elsa said, "that we can't go back to the lodge for a while."

Charlie laughed and put his hand on her shoulder. "You always were a smart one," he said. "What else have you figured out?"

"I haven't figured out a thing," she said. "But you're all moving around here like snails, when we could have this place slicked up and be straight off to bed in no time."

"I guess we'd better do something else, then," Nancy said with a laugh. "How about sitting around the campfire and singing songs?"

It took some coaxing, but Nancy finally got all of her friends in lawn chairs around the dying coals of the fire. After a few choruses of "Oh! Susannah" and "Red River Valley," everyone began to relax.

"Thank you for a great barbecue," Nancy said to Charlie and Rachel when a half hour had gone by. "Now let's go check our trap."

Charlie and Rachel carried buckets of water from a nearby horse trough to drown the fire. Then, with armloads of bowls and platters, the group started casually up the driveway toward the lodge.

Once inside, the girls hurried to the kitchen to deposit dirty dishes.

"You detectives run along now," Elsa said. "I'll take care of the dishes."

"Thanks, Elsa," Rachel said. "I'll make it up to you tomorrow."

Nancy, George, Rachel, and Charlie gathered around the coatrack by the front door.

Charlie reached into the pocket of his soiled jacket and pulled out the map.

"It wasn't stolen," Rachel said, sounding disappointed.

"Let's find out if it was read," Nancy said. She brought a piece of white paper from the desk and placed it on the floor.

Charlie carefully unfolded the map over the paper and shook it gently. The black sand was gone!

15

An Explosive Situation

"Someone's read the map, all right," Nancy said. "Now we have to find out who."

"I'm putting this in a safe place right now." Charlie refolded the map and started toward his office. "It really will make a nice addition to the display, don't you think?"

"That's a good idea," Nancy agreed. "We'll use my copy from now on."

Nancy glanced at her watch. "Our thief may be watching to make sure we all go to bed. Let's try to get a few hours' sleep. We'll meet back here at three A.M. That should give us time to get to the canyon before first light, right?"

"Right," Charlie said. "And I think I'll call the sheriff and let him know what we're up to, just in case."

As they walked back to their cabin, George said

to Nancy, "It's strange not having Bess here with us."

"I know," Nancy said with a sigh. "But I'm glad the doctor kept her at the hospital overnight. She needs her rest, and no one here is going to get much."

"That's for sure. I just wish I were sleepy now," George said. "I can't stop wondering if we're really going to find a gold mine tomorrow."

"And who else will be there," Nancy said as the two of them climbed into their bunks. "I still have a feeling there are some surprises left in this mystery."

"I think it's Tyler," George said. "Maybe Maddie and Pete are both helping him."

"Maybe," Nancy said, just before she drifted off to sleep.

A few hours later Nancy awoke with a start, quickly hitting the button to turn off her small travel alarm clock. She reached for the flashlight that she had placed under her pillow earlier. As she climbed out of bed, Nancy flashed the light on George's bunk. Her dark-haired friend was still sound asleep.

"Wake up, it's time." Nancy shook George gently.

"Huh? What's going . . . oh, right." George opened her eyes, slowly remembering why her friend was shaking her at three o'clock in the morning.

130

"It's that time already?" she said. "I feel as if I just got to sleep."

"It's that time," Nancy assured George, handing her jeans and a shirt. "We'd better hurry. The others will be here soon."

Nancy and George dressed in the dark and sat silently, waiting for a knock on the door. It was only a few minutes until they heard a gentle rapping.

"Rachel? Charlie? Is that you?" Nancy said softly through the closed door.

"Yes," she heard Charlie answer. "Are you ready?"

Nancy opened the door of the cabin, and she and George stepped out into the moonlight. She saw that Rachel was carrying a large flashlight, which she hadn't turned on, and Charlie had a walkie-talkie.

"I'm taking this in case we need to contact the sheriff," Charlie explained. "I've already asked him to be ready to help about the time the sun comes up."

"Good idea," Nancy said. She looked down the driveway. Both Tyler's cabin and Pete's house were completely dark.

The three girls followed Charlie to the jeep and climbed in. He had moved it to the driveway side of the barn, and Nancy noticed it was pointing down-hill.

"Hold on," Charlie whispered when everyone was seated. He released the parking brake, and the open jeep began to roll slowly down the hill. He steered it onto the driveway and let it bounce along in silence until they were almost to the main road.

When Charlie finally turned on the engine, the jeep was far enough away from the cabins and Pete's house to keep from disturbing any of the guests. They continued along the dusty road, with only the moon and stars to light their way.

Charlie shifted into low gear when they drew near Maddie's bird hospital.

"Do you think she heard us?" George asked when they were past.

"I don't know. We were pretty quiet," Nancy said.

"If she did, she probably thought we were just 'some fool city folks,'" Charlie said, mimicking Maddie's voice.

George and Nancy laughed, but Rachel just looked out at the trees going by. Nancy guessed she was still worried that Maddie might show up at the mine site when morning came.

It took another twenty minutes to drive through the dark to the end of the old logging road. Nancy and Rachel jumped out of the jeep and used their flashlights to find a path through the trees to a good hiding place. Charlie parked the jeep behind some large granite boulders. Then the group started up the trail to Prospector's Canyon.

The hike was even more difficult in the dark. Rachel led the way, warning the others when she saw a rock or tree root in the path. Even so, the girls often tripped. The loose rocks seemed to jump out at them from the path, making the darkness seem like an enemy. Even Nancy was feeling a little shaky by the time they finally arrived at the mouth of the canyon.

Castle Rock looked sinister in the darkness, hanging over the trail like a black shadow in the starlit sky. Occasionally Nancy motioned to the others for quiet, and for a few moments no one moved. Nancy listened for the rattle of rocks being kicked on the trail, or the swish of a tree branch that would tell her another person was in the canyon. She heard only the eerie call of an owl piercing the still night air.

"How long till dawn?" Nancy whispered to Rachel.

"Maybe an hour," Rachel answered.

"Let's make the most of the darkness while we can," Nancy said.

They followed Miner's Creek up the canyon until they reached the open hillside, where Nancy, George, and Rachel had found the signs of digging earlier. Nancy and Rachel shined their flashlights up toward the cliffs. The beams revealed a field mouse scampering over the rocks. It froze for a moment, then made a dash for the bushes.

"I don't think anyone is here," Rachel said.

The girls and Charlie followed Rachel up to the cliffs, and Nancy pulled out her map. Using Rachel's flashlight, they studied the rocks all along the edge of the cliffs.

"There isn't anything like what's shown on the map," Rachel said.

"Could we be in the wrong place?" George asked.

"I don't think so," Rachel said slowly. "I know this canyon, and there isn't any other place with the open hillside and the cliffs like this. This has to be the spot."

"Even if the mine had been buried, I don't know how we'd ever find it," Charlie said. "The last person who tried didn't seem to have much luck." He gestured to the empty holes on the hillside. "I guess Jeremiah's gold mine is going to stay a mystery."

Rachel sighed. "If we can catch whoever's been trying to destroy the retreat, I'll be happy," she said, but her voice sounded discouraged.

Nancy was disappointed, too. If a mine did exist, it had been well covered. Perhaps in the light it would show up. Or maybe it was all just a story. But the map was convincing. It looked old, the paper yellowed with time. And why would Jeremiah go to the trouble of hiding the map if it weren't the key to the mother lode? Nancy wondered.

"Rachel's right," she said at last. "We can still make this a success by catching our culprit. Let's find a place to hide."

Charlie and the girls followed the cliffs to a spot overgrown with heavy brush and trees. They settled down there and waited for morning.

Time seemed to drag by. After nearly an hour of

staying still in their rocky hideaway, Nancy wished she could stretch her legs. She knew the others were probably feeling the same way, but no one complained. Nancy closed her eyes, trying to imagine herself in a big pool of warm water, but the image did little to soothe the cramps in her legs. When Nancy opened her eyes, Rachel was pointing down the hill. A figure in light-colored clothes and a cowboy hat had just come into view on the trail.

Nancy was instantly alert. She looked around and saw that George and Charlie were also intently watching the figure below them. Nancy could see that the person was carrying some sort of bag over one shoulder. Her eyes were riveted to the figure.

To the east, the sky had turned a bright violet as the sun rose over the horizon. A few gray-edged clouds floated through the sunrise, and the canyon took on a cheery, pink tone. The silhouette climbing the hill cast the only dark shadow on the otherwise beautiful summer morning.

Nancy could tell from the figure's height and build that they were watching a man. She was relieved, for Rachel's sake, that it wasn't Maddie climbing the hill. She wished that the person would take off the cowboy hat so they could see his face. They would just have to wait.

The man climbed to the small clump of bushes where Nancy had found the tools and pouch on their earlier visit. He leaned over and pulled out the shovel and pick, then opened the duffel bag. He stopped and looked down into the bag he'd been carrying, as though considering what to do next. With his right hand he pulled a handkerchief from his hip pocket. His left hand reached to the brim of his hat, and as he slipped it off his head, Nancy's eyes widened in surprise. She looked over at the others, who appeared equally shocked.

"It's B.D. Eastham," Rachel whispered. "I don't believe it."

For a moment Nancy didn't believe it, either, but then the pieces of the puzzle began to fall into place. On the day she and her friends had arrived, B.D. had heard them talk about stopping in town on the way from the airport, so he had had time to set the fire. He had even suggested the place to eat. B.D. had also been at the retreat on the day of the explosion and the runaway jeep, and on the night the lodge was ransacked. He even knew what time they had planned their trail ride to Prospector's Canyon on the day the rattlesnakes were put on the trail. Getting around the retreat would have been easy for B.D., too, Nancy realized. The forest provided good cover, and if anyone did see him, B.D. could just play the part of a visiting friend.

"This has to be a mistake," Charlie whispered. "We've caught a friend instead of a fiend."

Nancy knew she would have to get something concrete on B.D. to convince Charlie and Rachel that their friend had tried to destroy the retreat. Thinking quickly, she motioned for the others to stay hidden. She had just one chance to prove the truth.

Nancy stepped out of the trees and started down the hill toward B.D.

"Beat me to it, I see," she said when she was about twenty feet from him.

B.D. whirled around to face Nancy, and she saw the surprise on his face. Then his expression turned to anger.

"Why did you follow me? I'm in no mood for games today," he said, reaching for his duffel bag.

"I didn't follow you. I followed this map." Nancy pulled her copy of Jeremiah's map from her pocket. "You've got one, too, right?"

B.D. hesitated. "It was nice of you to find the map for me," he said with a shrug. "I didn't have much luck going through that display myself."

"It looks to me as if the best plan now is to share the gold," Nancy said. "I suspect there's plenty for both of us, anyway."

"Not a chance," B.D. said. His eyes had hardened, and an evil grin came over his face. "Not with you or anybody. I've been working on this for years. I'm sick of flying tourists in and out of that dusty airport. The land sale almost ruined everything, but it won't matter now. All I have to do is find the mine, get what I can carry, and fly straight out of here. There are plenty of sunny beaches in South America where they'll never find me. It looks like *you're* my only problem."

"I don't think so," Nancy said, deciding to try another angle. "I already looked for the mine. It's not where the map shows it. You've done all this

137

work for nothing—unless you know something I don't."

"Now, how could that be, when you're such a big detective?" B.D. said sarcastically. "You found my assay report in the meadow. Couldn't you figure out that a rock slide buried the old mine years ago?"

"So you did start the fire?" Nancy asked.

"That's right," B.D. said casually. He reached into his pocket and pulled out a black cigarette lighter, smiling at Nancy as he flicked a flame to life. "Nothing to it," he said. "The dry grass lights easily, and this handy lighter leaves no evidence behind."

"What did you have assayed, anyway?" Nancy asked. She knew she would have to keep B.D. talking.

B.D. shrugged. "A piece of ore, just like Charlie's. I found it about where you're standing," he said. "It was full of gold."

Nancy took a step closer. "If you know I found the assay report, you must have been the one who broke into our cabin and sent Bess to the hospital," she said boldly. Her anger was building, but she knew she had to stay in control of her emotions.

"She got in my way. That's a dangerous thing to do," B.D. said.

Nancy understood his threat but pressed on with her questions.

"Have you ever heard of the Nature Preservation League?" she asked.

B.D. gave a grim laugh. "I'm its only member,"

he said. "I was hoping Charlie would stop negotiating with the government so I'd have time."

"And were you the mail carrier who lost Charlie's letters to Senator Callihan?" Nancy asked.

"You are clever," B.D. said, looking surprised. "I couldn't believe my luck when Charlie asked me to take those letters to town. It was so easy to drop them in the wrong box—you know, the garbage can."

Just then Charlie marched down the hill. "How could you throw away our friendship for a bunch of rocks?" he bellowed, his face red with anger. His strides were long and quick, even over the rocky ground. Rachel and George had come out of hiding, too, and they had to hurry to keep up with Charlie as the three of them approached B.D.

B.D.'s evil smile vanished when he saw Charlie. For a moment Nancy thought she saw a hint of sorrow in his eyes, but then the glint of greed returned.

"Not rocks—gold," B.D. said. "And our friendship was nothing compared to being rich."

"But you hurt people!" Rachel yelled from behind Charlie. "You hit Bess, and that trick with the snakes was dangerous to everyone on the ride. And I can't believe what you did to my salmon beds." Rachel choked back a sob, and her grandfather put his arm around her.

"I'm calling the sheriff," Charlie said.

"I don't think so," B.D. said calmly. He pulled a

stick of dynamite from his duffel bag. Nancy could see it had an extra-short fuse. "This will stop you," he said.

He waved the loaded dynamite stick in one hand and the lighter in the other.

Rachel and George stepped backward, closer to the cliffs. Nancy thought fast. There had to be a way to stop B.D.

"Go ahead, call the sheriff," he said. "I'll blow you all away and still have enough dynamite to blast the mine."

Charlie hadn't moved since B.D. had begun to wave the dynamite. Charlie's face was locked in a determined frown as he said, "Sorry, B.D. I'm calling your bluff." He switched on the walkie-talkie and contacted the sheriff.

"You're wrong about that," B.D. said. "Where there's gold involved, I'll do whatever I have to do."

B.D. lit the fuse. It sparkled and smoked as Nancy and the others watched in horror.

"Run for cover!" Nancy hollered. She made a dash toward some rocks. George, Rachel, and Charlie were right behind her. They were still several yards away when B.D. tossed the dynamite. It lit right in front of Nancy, falling out of reach between two rocks. The fuse was growing shorter by the second!

16

A Golden Opportunity

"Hurry!" Nancy yelled. With flying steps she ran away from the dynamite and dived behind a huge boulder. Charlie and Rachel were close behind her, and George rolled to the ground beside them just as a huge blast rocked the canyon wall. Nancy, George, Rachel, and Charlie wrapped their arms over their heads and huddled close to the boulder as bits of dirt and rock rained down on them.

When the worst seemed to be past, Nancy looked over at her friends. They were covered with dirt, but otherwise seemed unhurt. She peeked over the rock in time to see B.D. running down the hill, carrying his duffel bag. Nancy hurdled over the rocks and ran after him. She had to keep him in sight until the deputies arrived.

The blast had given him a long head start. He was at the bottom of the hill and on the trail before she was halfway down. B.D. was making good time, and it looked to Nancy as if he might escape, despite all her efforts. She was still half-running, half-sliding down the hill when she heard the whir of a helicopter overhead.

She looked up. A four-man copter was coming over the ridge into Prospector's Canyon. She could see a sheriff's department symbol on the side.

As the copter hovered over the trail, the barrel of a rifle appeared from an open door. Another deputy produced a bullhorn.

From where she stood, Nancy had trouble making out the words. But she saw B.D. drop his duffel bag and raise his arms in the air. The helicopter began to descend, and Nancy felt a great sense of relief. She headed back up the hill to check on her friends.

"Come look at this!" George called down to her from the base of the cliffs.

Nancy hurried to George, Rachel, and Charlie, who were standing around a small opening in the rocks, at a spot where the dynamite had exploded.

"Do you think it's the mine?" Rachel asked.

"It could be," Nancy said. "Let's find out."

She grabbed B.D.'s shovel and began to remove the rest of the loose gravel and dirt. Charlie used the pick to loosen some large rocks, and George and Rachel helped to roll them out of the way. Soon they uncovered the opening to a cave large enough to walk through. The walls and ceiling were mostly dirt, with a few large boulders hanging down. They looked as though they might fall at any minute. The dirt was moist, and the air coming out of the cave smelled musty.

"It's Jeremiah's mine!" Rachel yelled.

Nancy took Rachel's flashlight and shone it into the opening.

"No one goes in," Charlie ordered. "It's too dangerous."

Nancy flashed the light onto the floor of the cave. Suddenly Rachel screamed and pointed.

Propped against a rock was a human skeleton, its clothes still clinging to its frame. Beside the skeleton was a set of leather saddlebags.

The girls and Charlie huddled around the entrance to the mine, gazing into the beam of light.

"Do you think it's Jeremiah?" George asked.

"Dead in his own mine," Charlie said, shaking his head. "I never would have guessed."

"Look at the saddlebags," Nancy said. "They look full, but of what?" Nancy looked at Charlie, remembering his warning. "I've got to get those saddlebags," she said. "I won't go any farther."

Charlie shrugged. "Could I stop you if I wanted to?" he asked. "Just be careful."

Nancy stepped carefully into the shaft. It took her only a few steps to get to the saddlebags. She lifted them up carefully. In the beam of her flashlight, she could see the initials *J.B.* stamped into the leather.

Nancy looked back at the skeleton and shook her head. They had found Jeremiah Benner!

Cautiously Nancy took the saddlebags back out into the open air. Charlie breathed a sigh of relief when Nancy stepped clear of the cave. Rachel clicked off her flashlight.

"Another mystery solved," Nancy said, showing the others the initials.

"These are heavy," George said, taking the saddlebags. "What's inside?"

"Let's find out," Nancy said. She unbuckled the strap. Inside the bags she found several pieces of rich gold ore and one large nugget, with a small amount of quartz still clinging to it. The gold had a dull shine in the morning sun. Nancy picked up the nugget and turned it over in her hand, then gave it to Charlie.

"Fool's gold?" she asked.

Charlie's hand dropped as he took the stone. He measured the weight of it in his palm and smiled broadly. "Real gold," he said at last. "It's too heavy to be anything else."

Rachel jumped into the air and shouted.

"I guess you're rich," George said, smiling broadly.

"We're going to celebrate tonight!" Charlie said, throwing his arms around Rachel.

It seemed like a short walk back to the jeep. Everyone took turns carrying the heavy saddlebags, chattering excitedly.

Just outside the lodge the group was met by Bess. The doctor had given her a clean bill of health and

144

released her from the hospital before breakfast. Elsa had brought her back to the retreat.

"I was hoping I wouldn't miss anything," Bess said. "But as soon as I realized you were gone, I knew it was too late."

Nancy and George filled her in on the events of the day. Bess gasped in horror when George told about the dynamite and finding the skeleton. Nancy explained how B.D. had confessed to all of the incidents at the retreat.

"I can't believe it was B.D.," she said. "I guess I'll have to apologize to Pete for thinking he took the quartz."

"What's that?" a voice said behind her. Pete had just walked up the road toward the lodge.

"I'm afraid I almost got you into trouble," Bess stammered. "I thought you took Charlie's quartz."

"Took it? I tried to return it," Pete said in surprise. "Shirley Kauffman gave it to me when I got back from checking fences two days ago. I put it on a shelf in the barn, behind a grain can. Then Tyler asked me to come look at some gold flecks he'd panned in the creek. It was just fool's gold, but it made me forget about Charlie's quartz. When I got back to the barn later, it was gone."

Rachel laughed. "Bess found the quartz. It's safe in Granddad's office," she said. "Bess also saw you talking to Tyler." Rachel explained why the girls had suspected Pete of stealing the ore and plotting

145

to destroy the retreat, and how B.D. had finally been arrested for the crimes.

"B.D. Eastham—arrested?" Pete said, surprised. He pushed his cowboy hat back and shook his head. "Are you sure there hasn't been some mistake?"

"Absolutely," Rachel said. She told him about B.D.'s confession.

"So, where's breakfast?" Bess asked as they headed into the lodge. "I bet Elsa has something delicious for us, and I've had enough of hospital food."

"You were only there for one meal," George teased.

"I know, but I couldn't stop thinking of you eating that delicious barbecued beef," she said.

Charlie met them at the door, saying he had just finished talking on the phone to the sheriff. B.D. was safely behind bars, Charlie reported, being held on suspicion of arson, attempted murder, and a number of other charges. He had already admitted everything to the sheriff.

"I also told the sheriff about the mine and Jeremiah Benner's remains," Charlie said. "He's sending his deputies back up to Prospector's Canyon."

After a large breakfast of pancakes and fruit, Nancy, Rachel, and George were all ready to catch up on their sleep.

"We'll have another barbecue again tonight,"

Charlie announced as they headed for their bunks. "And this time, no spilling barbecue sauce on the host!"

The sun was just going down when everyone was gathered around the campfire again, along with the other guests, Maddie, and Pete.

After hearing how B.D. had been discovered with a duffel bag full of explosives, Maddie explained that she had found the blasting cap in Prospector's Canyon. "I didn't want to tell you I'd been there," Maddie said. "Especially after you said you were looking for someone coming in the back way to the retreat. You see, there's a golden eagle nest at the back end of the canyon, and I had been out checking on it."

Nancy asked about Rocky, the eagle.

"He's doing better," she said. Then she leaned close to Nancy. "I think I've got a line on a grant to build a new hospital. I've been talking to Tyler Nelson this week, and he says the senator may be able to help."

"That is, if no one sics the sheriff on me," Tyler teased, leaning over Nancy's shoulder.

"Sorry," Nancy said. "I really did think it was you at first, Tyler."

"Charlie told me B.D. lied about when I flew into town. If you'd finished your snooping when you were in my cabin, you might have seen in my appointment book that I got here *after* you, not before."

"How did you know I was in your cabin?" Nancy asked sheepishly.

Tyler grinned. "Charlie told me. He wanted to know about the letter from the preservation group. I had taken the one from his desk and made a copy. I saw it there one day, and I wanted to check out the competition. I found out it was a bogus operation, too. That was as far as I got. Except that I did learn not to send mail with B.D. It kept getting lost. But I never made the connection between all the near-disasters and the gold. It took you to do that, Nancy."

"I just wish I'd figured out it was B.D. sooner," Nancy said.

"He's the last person anyone would have guessed," Tyler said. "I don't think Charlie and Rachel would believe it now if you hadn't convinced them with that daring plan of yours.

"There's one thing I still don't understand," Tyler continued. "Why was Jeremiah's skeleton in the mine?"

"He must have been caught in a rock slide," Nancy said. "That hillside is unstable. Maybe, if Charlie's dad, Cyrus, had known where Jeremiah was, he could have been saved. So I guess, in a way, it was his own greed that killed him."

"Just like it was greed that got B.D.," Tyler said. "Greed and your good detective work."

Nancy was embarrassed to have one of her suspects complimenting her. She thanked Tyler and was going to get herself more lemonade when Charlie tapped a glass with his fork and began to speak.

"I have an announcement," he said. "As you all know by now, we've had some pretty unusual guests at the Highland Retreat this week. And they've solved a couple of old mysteries. So I have a special souvenir for each of them."

Charlie handed Nancy, George, and Bess each a gold chain with a pendant of gold-veined quartz.

"Maddie told me about a jewelry artist in Eagle Point who works with stones," he said. "While you were asleep, he made these up. He also told me that gold ore is so unusual, and so pretty, that it may be worth more than the gold by itself. We're going into partnership. He's going to make 'Highland Gold' jewelry."

"It's beautiful," Bess said, admiring her necklace. "I bet soon we'll be seeing it in stores in River Heights."

All three of the girls gave their hosts a special thank-you for the unusual souvenirs.

"What about the land sale?" Nancy asked.

"We're renegotiating that," Tyler Nelson said.

"Yes," Charlie added. "I've decided to will the land to the state for a wildlife refuge. In the meantime, Pete and Elsa and I will keep running it as a retreat. That way, Rachel can come back to visit her salmon anytime she wants."

"And tomorrow I'm hiring a contractor to help fix the spawning beds," Rachel said. "It took me all summer to build that dam, but I bet a professional can do it in a few days.''

Nancy looked over the gathering around the campfire. It had been one wild week, not at all the relaxing vacation she and her friends had had in mind. But it had definitely been worthwhile to help Charlie keep his retreat and send Rachel to college.

"I think the best part is yet to come," Bess said.

"What's that?" Nancy asked.

"With our pilot in jail, we really *will* have to take the train back to Seattle. I'm sure I'll like the scenery better from ground level."

Nancy laughed and put her arm around Bess's shoulder. "I'm glad B.D. confessed, or I might have thought you framed him to avoid that plane ride back," she said.

As the group's laughter died down, Nancy heard a coyote howl. She was glad that Highland Retreat was safe at last, but most of all she was glad to be celebrating with such good friends.